Amy
Enjoy
Wet !

BELOW

Deck

TARA SIVEC

[signature] xo

Below Deck
Copyright © 2017 Tara Sivec
Print Edition

Disclaimer
This is a work of adult fiction. The author does not endorse or condone
any of the behavior enclosed within. The subject matter may not be
appropriate for minors. All trademarks and copyrighted items mentioned
are the property of their respective owners.

Cover Design by Tara Sivec

Edits by Holly Malgieri from Holly's Red Hot Reviews
www.hollysredhotreviews.com

Interior Design by Paul Salvette, BB eBooks
bbebooksthailand.com

DEDICATION

For Kelley Johnson. You'll never read this since you're a big Bravo TV star, but thanks for the inspiration anyway. I appreciate you for more than just being a lovely piece of eye candy. Probably. Maybe. Okay fine. Thanks for being really pretty and stuff.

TABLE OF CONTENTS

GLOSSARY OF TERMS

Bosun: Also known as a Petty Officer or a qualified member of the deck department, is the senior most member of the deck department and is responsible for the components of a ship's hull and supervises the other members of the ship's deck department.

Chief Steward/Chief Stew: The senior unlicensed crew member working in the steward's department of a ship. The chief steward directs, instructs, and assigns personnel performing such functions as preparing and serving meals. Moreover, the steward oversees cleaning and maintaining officers' quarters and steward department areas; and receiving, issuing, and inventorying stores.

Port: The left-hand side of or direction from a vessel, facing forward.

Starboard: The side of a ship that is on the right when one is facing forward.

Bridge: The room or platform from which the ship can be commanded.

Wheelhouse: The small enclosed parts of a bridge that historically held the ship's wheel.

Main Salon: The main social area of a passenger ship.

Galley: The kitchen area of a ship.

Crew Mess: Located below deck, this is the area where crew members eat and socialize.

Crew Pantry: Typically, a small kitchenette off the galley where stews can make drinks, wash dishes, and conduct other small kitchen tasks separate from what the chef does in the galley.

Engine Room: A lower compartment for housing the propulsion system of a ship.

CHAPTER 1

⚓

Declan

"DECLAN, DECLAN."
My name crackles over the radio attached to the belt of my cargo shorts, and I drop the rag I was using to wipe down the railings on the upper deck. Rolling my shoulders to work out the kinks from the grueling process of getting the 154-foot yacht, *Helios*, ready for its next clients, I close my eyes and tilt my head up towards the sun as I unclip the radio and bring it up to my mouth.

"Go for Declan," I speak, depressing the talk button.

I enjoy a few peaceful seconds of having the Caribbean sun on my face while I'm standing still long enough to appreciate it, instead of racing all over this ship busting my ass. The smell of salt water on the light breeze cools my sweaty skin and the gentle lap of waves against the side of the ship makes me smile, even though I'm fucking exhausted after waking up at the ass crack of dawn this morning.

Working on a yacht is the hardest job I've ever had in my thirty-two years, and I've had many. Long hours, shitty pay, dealing with rich, and sometimes famous, assholes who treat you like dirt while you wait on them hand and foot. Putting up with a captain who expects nothing but the best from his crew and rips you a new asshole if you can't read his mind and anticipate all of his needs for running a smooth ship. Being away from home for long stretches of time, sleeping in a bunk that's smaller than my bathroom at home, suffering through all the high school drama and bullshit that goes on within the crew, then waking up and starting the process all over again when it's time for a new group of clients.

Like I said, it's the hardest job I've ever had, but it's the best damn job there is. How many people can say they work on one of the largest luxury yachts and get to spend all their time floating through crystal clear water, island hopping, and seeing the world? Besides, it's not like I plan on being a little whipping bitch for these rich dicks forever. I have a plan, and nothing is getting in the way of it.

"I need you, Ashley, and Marcel down in the crew mess in five," Captain Michael barks through the radio, ending my few minutes of peace.

"Copy that," I reply before clipping the radio back on my belt.

I take a minute to stare out over the railing at the island of St. Thomas from where we're docked at the Crown Bay Marina, the view still amazing me even though I've been here a hundred times in the last four years that I've been a yachtie. With one last deep breath, I head inside the ship, through the formal dining room to the galley, and take the narrow staircase down to the crew quarters. Leaving the guest area of the ship and entering into the peasant, a.k.a. crew area is so pathetic you can't help but laugh. Where up top is filled with dark, shiny mahogany wood, fancy couches, expensive artwork, bedrooms the size of a small home, and stone shower tile imported from fucking Egypt or something, *we* eat, sleep, shit, shower and shave in a tiny maze of hallways where you have to turn sideways to get through them. Our wood is fake laminate that a baby can punch through, and our artwork consists of hand-drawn dicks and tits that my co-worker and friend, Ben Lucas, decided to hang all around our table nook to brighten things up down here.

With an annoyed frown at all the opulence up top and the shit quarters the crew has, I vow for the hundredth time that when I'm the captain of my own yacht, I will make sure the crew is taken care of and not shit on all the time.

Lost in thought as I stare at my feet and rush

through the tiny hallway taking me past the crew bunks and into the crew mess, I slam into someone quickly exiting their bunk. We both let out an *"Oof"* and a few choice curse words. Looking back and forth between the guy in front of me hastily zipping up his khaki cargo shorts while tucking in his navy blue polo, and the bunk he just exited, I sigh and run my hand through the already messy spikes of hair on my head.

"Dude, how many times have I told you not to shit where you eat?"

Ben laughs softly, pulling the door to Jessica Miller, one of the three stewardess' bunks, closed behind him before giving me a smirk.

"Do you really expect me to remain celibate the entire five months of this charter season? That's just inhuman," he explains with a slow shake of his head.

"No, I expect you to get your piece of ass *off* the ship, with locals or tourists, like a normal person. I'm not playing referee between you two when shit goes south and she turns into a psycho," I tell him, lowering my voice so Jessica doesn't hear me talking about her on the other side of the door.

It's not like I know Jessica all that well since she's new to the crew this season and we've only been at it for three weeks. She seems like a nice enough girl and eager to help wherever she's needed—fresh out of college and wanting to see the world before she settles down with a landlocked career. But I made the mistake

4

of getting off with a co-worker several drunken times over the years, and now I'm paying for it. They all seem nice enough until they have selective hearing, and when you say, *"This is just sex because we've been at sea for four months and we're both really horny,"* she assumes you said, *"I will love you forever and we'll get married and have babies and live happily-ever-after."*

"Hey, it's not my fault you fucked up when you were a newbie and screwed the Chief Stew. And then did it again and again the last few charters you worked with her. It's also not my fault she's excellent at her job and being a stage five clinger to your ass isn't enough cause to get her fired. Besides, Jessica gives the most mind numbing blow—"

"Are you boys going to stand around gossiping all day? The captain is waiting for us," Ashley Padgett, Chief Stew and the stage five clinger in question, huffs out irritably from behind me in the small hallway.

Ben snorts and I punch him in the arm before turning around to face her, refusing to return the seductive smile she tries to give me when our eyes meet.

As the Chief Stewardess, Ashley is in charge of the two other stewardesses that work beneath her—Jessica the new girl, and Zoe Ledford, a pretty cool chick I've worked with a few times on different charters. Ashley's job entails everything that has to do with the interior of the ship from cleaning the guest quarters, to serving their food and drinks and waiting on them hand and foot. Me being the Bosun on the ship, and in charge of the deckhands and everything to do with the exterior, I'm forced to work closely with Ashley to make sure nothing falls through the cracks and the charter guests have nothing but a perfect experience when they're on the *Helios*. A job that has become much more difficult ever since I slept with her one night four years ago during my first charter season after a few too many rum and cokes on our night off. And then I proceeded to make that same mistake a handful of times since then. I had been so busy learning my way around a boat that I didn't have time to go off to the mainland and find a local to hook up with. My dick was about to explode from non-use, and Ashley was more than willing to ease my pain. One night of drunk fucking led to a few more nights of drunk fucking, which always led to me waking up the next morning, swearing I'd never do it again, which has resulted in several years of hell.

I finally told her at the end of last season's charter that there would be no more hooking up between us. I didn't need the hassle and I didn't need the baggage, working with someone who thought me getting drunk and horny meant I wanted to spend the rest of my life with her. To say she didn't take it well would be putting it mildly. Three weeks and three different sets of charter guests into *this* season and I've almost jumped ship a few times.

"Let's go, Decky," Ashley practically purrs. The

childish and stupid fucking nickname she won't stop using makes me break out in a cold sweat, as does the way she closes the distance between us in the narrow hallway, wrapping her hand around my bicep and pressing her fake tits against me.

I hear another snort from Ben before I untangle my arm from her hold and move away from her, grinding my teeth together to stop myself from telling her to cut this shit out and stop calling me fucking *Decky*. I cannot afford to start an argument with this woman twenty-one-days into the charter season. Not just because we still have to work together day and night for seventeen more weeks, but because Captain Michael sees all and hears all. A screaming match between two of his chief crew members will not earn me any brownie points and will definitely make him change his mind about possibly mentoring me to become a captain. The one and only thing I give a shit about right now.

"Ben, radio Eddie and have him help you do a final check on all the water toys. Make sure everything is accounted for, clean, and in the right spot," I tell him as we both turn sideways so I can squeeze past him and get to captain before he has a shit fit because I'm late.

"I radioed him four times a little bit ago and he didn't answer. Dipshit probably left it on a counter somewhere again."

I stop in my tracks, causing Ashley to run into the back of me and giving her yet another excuse to put her hands on me to stop herself from falling. I ignore her giggles and the patting of her hands as she smooths down the parts of my shirt she grabbed ahold of when I stopped suddenly, and look back over my shoulder at Ben.

Just like Jessica, Eddie Merrill is new to our crew this season and he, too, just graduated from college and wanted to see the world before he got a job on land. Unlike Jessica, Eddie is dumber than a box of rocks and you have to tell him something fifteen times before it finally sinks in. Like the fact that you never, ever go anywhere on this ship without your radio. You eat with it, you sleep with it, you fuck with it, and you shit with it.

"Don't worry about it, get to your meeting," Ben tells me with a wave of his hand. "I'll find Eddie's radio, find *him*, and then shove it up his ass so he doesn't have a choice but to keep it with him at all times."

Ben gives me a thumb's up, I give him a nod, and then turn back around and move as quickly away from Ashley as possible.

Ben and I met four years ago when we were both hired to work on the *Helios*. It was my first time working on a boat this size, but Ben had been working on luxury yachts ever since he graduated high school and, like me, couldn't afford college and couldn't figure out what the fuck he wanted to do with his life. It took me ten years of bouncing between factory jobs and constructions jobs, each one more miserable than the last, before I finally figured out what my passion was. We've worked together on the *Helios* every charter season, and since we both live in Florida, we hang out when we're not at sea as well. When I was promoted to Bosun two seasons ago, I was worried it would royally fuck up our friendship since Ben would be forced to take orders from me. Luckily, Ben is the most laid back guy you'd ever meet. He loves his job, does what he's told, and gives zero fucks that I'm the one telling him what to do. He's always been content as a deckhand and has no desire to move up the ranks or do anything else with his life. He's known since day one that I want more and I'll do whatever it takes to get there, and he was genuinely happy for me when I got the promotion.

When I make it into the crew mess, I see Marcel Petit, the chef on the *Helios*, already seated, tapping his fingers on the table and glaring at me in annoyance. He's the same age as me, grew up in France, trained in Paris at the Cordon Bleu, understands English, but has never, in all the charters I've worked with him, ever uttered anything but French curse words. At least I'm assuming that's what's coming out of his mouth when he's banging around the galley, slamming pots and pans and screaming words I don't understand.

I squeeze behind the ten-person corner nook table, sliding across the bench seat and around to the back of the table next to Marcel just as Captain Michael enters

9

from the stairs that lead up to the bridge. Ashley quickly scrambles into a chair across from us, immediately donning an air of professionalism with a lift of her chin and her hands clasped neatly in front of her on the table, knowing full well she has to be on her best behavior in front of the captain.

"The Armstrong family," Captain Michael starts right in without a greeting, tossing each of us a stapled packet of computer printouts.

The packets fly across the smooth surface of the table and we all have to slap our hands down on top of them to stop the pages from falling into our laps. We quietly flip through the dossier on tomorrow's charter guests as the captain takes a seat on the other side of me, pulling a pen out of the breast pocket of his white button down uniform shirt and jotting a few notes on his own packet before he continues.

"Our main charter guest is Mark Armstrong, early sixties, independent software developer who worked out of his basement until he made his first hundred million selling a dating app," the captain continues as Ashley and I stare at the small square photo of Mark Armstrong next to his short bio.

Each guest for tomorrow's charter has pretty much the same information—photo, relationship to the main charter guest (the one who booked it and paid for it), dietary restrictions, special requests for food and activities, and what they do for a living. Mostly, the main charter guest is the only one who actually makes money, all the rest are just along for the ride to act like entitled assholes and spend all of his or her money. Which seems to be the case, yet again, for tomorrow's guests as I listen and read along with Captain Michael as he ticks off facts about the people Mark Armstrong is bringing with him to abuse us for the next ten days.

Allyson Drake-Swanson-Armstrong, early forties and Mark Armstrong's new bride as of a few weeks ago.

Judging by the number of hyphens in her name, I'm going to assume Mark won't be her last husband, and the poor schmucks she was married to before him are probably the ones responsible for all the plastic surgery she's had on her face.

I listen half-assed to the captain explain the rest of the guests, flipping ahead to the last page. My jaw drops open at the photo staring back at me. I've seen my fill of hot women by working on a yacht for four years. And since they're *rich*, hot women, they can afford to be nipped and tucked and lifted in all the right places to make sure their assets are top of the line. I've seen hot women in evening gowns, I've seen hot women in thong bikinis, I've seen hot women in sundresses with their tits practically falling out, and I've seen hot women lying on the upper sundeck with nothing but the Caribbean sun covering them.

What I've *never* seen before is a woman who could make my jaw drop and find it impossible to tear my eyes away from her photo and the information printed next to it.

Mackenzie Armstrong, late twenties, daughter to Mark Armstrong.

Graduated top of her class at NYU in graphic design, immediately went to work for her father and sits on the board of several of his charities. No dietary restrictions, and her special requests are to drive a jet ski and swim with dolphins.

Sits on the board for several charities is code for, "Doesn't really have a job other than spending daddy's money throwing fancy parties."

Even knowing this information, I still can't stop staring at her picture. Long dark hair with a few strands blowing across her face, light blue eyes the color of the ocean water outside, full, gorgeous lips and a dimple in one cheek as she smiles the biggest smile at whoever took the photo. Maybe I'm struck dumb because these guest bios usually contain professional headshots against boring photo studio backdrops, or stupid ass selfies people take in front of the mirror, like the ones the rest of the Armstrong clan used. This picture of Mackenzie Armstrong is candid and *real* and someone took it when she was mid-laugh, which lights up her entire face.

"These people have more money than God, so do your jobs, don't fuck anything up, and hopefully we'll get a nice tip at the end of the charter," Captain Michael finishes, pushing himself up off the bench and exiting the room.

His words dump a bucket of cold water on my libido, and I shove the packet away from me in annoyance. Another snobby, entitled group of guests who can afford to throw away $200,000 a week to charter a yacht and who'll treat the crew like shit, just like all the other guests I've encountered in the last four years.

There are a lot of rules in yachting, but nothing more sacred than the holy trinity—never go anywhere without your radio, never shit where you eat, and never, ever cross the line with a guest.

It's not like it matters that one little photo of her made my dick hard. She's still one of *them*, born with a silver spoon in her mouth and wouldn't know anything about a hard day's work if it smacked her in the face, and *completely* off limits.

Sliding out from behind the table, I leave Ashley and Marcel alone to discuss the menu, knowing the exact moment when Marcel reads that the guests are requesting a twelve course dinner for one night, each course to be brought out exactly fifteen minutes apart, with no seafood, red meat, or anything with the colors green or red in it. And that isn't even the strangest request we've ever gotten on a charter.

"Va te faire enculer!" Marcel screams, pounding his fist against the top of the table as I hear Ashley try to calm him, and I move faster down the hall to go find Ben and Eddie.

Go fuck yourself. At least I know *that* string of words from Marcel, because he uses it the most and I made a point of Googling the translation a while back. I have a feeling Marcel and I will be using that phrase a lot over the next ten days.

Him, every time someone has a special food request, and me, every time I have to deal with the hot, but spoiled Mackenzie Armstrong and the rest of her highbrow family.

I have a job to do, and I'm going to do it, end of story. One pretty face isn't going to distract me from my goals.

CHAPTER 2

⚓

Mackenzie

"UGH, WHY IS so hot? My skin is practically melting and it's putting wrinkles in my Dolce and Gabbana sundress."

I roll my eyes as I walk a safe distance down the dock behind my stepsister, Arianna. A safe distance is necessary because if I have to listen to her complain about one more thing on this trip, I'm going to rip the blonde hair extensions, she spent way too much money on, out of her head and toss them into the North Atlantic.

"Aren't there any clouds in this Godforsaken place? A little shade would be nice," Allyson, Arianna's mother and my new stepmonster adds, hooking her elbow around her daughter's so the two of them can form a human chain of twin, blonde hair extension misery.

I watch their perfect, fake hair swirl around their

shoulders and down their backs when the ocean breeze moves through it, stare at their long, smooth and shiny legs fresh from yesterday's wax at the most high-end spa on St. Thomas, and glare at the matching Hermès Birkin bags dangling off their elbows that aren't linked together. As if going on this family vacation to celebrate the farce of a marriage between Allyson and my father wasn't asinine enough, and something my father should not be wasting his money on after my most recent, eye-opening meeting with his corporate attorneys and accountants, Allyson and Arianna have spent every waking moment since we landed here two days ago spending an ungodly amount of money on clothing, shoes, jewelry, and purses.

Things they don't need. Things they already have tucked away in their huge walk-in-closets back at my father's house in New York, but insist are "So last season." Things my father absolutely *cannot* afford right now.

"Just say the word and I'll trip one of them. Maybe even add in a swift kick to the gut for good luck."

I forget about my father's money troubles for a few seconds when my best friend, Brooke Talbot, leans in and whispers in my ear as we get closer to the end of the dock where the luxury yacht Allyson insisted on chartering for ten days is docked. As soon as my father told me we'd all be going on their honeymoon together, I spent a week trying to convince him that it wasn't a good idea for him to be spending so much money on a trip like this right now. It was seven days of me wasting my breath. My arguments and insistence that he cancel the trip fell on the deaf ears of a man who'd been single since my mother died when I was ten, and was currently blinded by love and wedded bliss.

Knowing there was nothing I could do to change my father's mind, I relented and begrudgingly agreed to the trip, but only if I could bring Brooke. There is no way I'd survive this hellish experience if she weren't by my side. Much to Allyson and Arianna's horror, since they can't stand my best friend, my father immediately agreed to my demands and insisted on paying Brooke's way. I let him go right ahead and add Brooke to our travel arrangements, knowing full well Brooke would *never* let anyone pay her way for anything, not even my father who loves her like a second daughter and has known her since wet met on our first day of kindergarten. As soon as I told Brooke what we were doing and to cancel all of her plans for the next two weeks, she wrote my father a check for her share of the trip and I immediately deposited it into his account.

"Do Hermès bags sink? If the blonde bimbos fall into the water, would they work like flotation devices or drag them to the bottom of the ocean, never to be seen or heard from again?" Brooke asks as we watch my father move between the two women and do his best to comfort them and get them to stop complaining about the heat for five minutes.

Considering it was Allyson's idea to come to the U.S. Virgin Islands, and she downright threw a childish hissy fit, complete with foot stomping and screaming when my father suggested something a little less tropical, you'd think she would have realized it might be a little hot in the Caribbean in the middle of the fucking summer.

"Sadly, I believe leather floats. But considering I can see the bottom of the ocean from here and it's probably not that deep, I don't think there's any chance of them drowning," I inform Brooke as we get to the end of the dock and stare at the giant boat that will be our home for the next ten days.

Brooke whistles as she looks the vessel over and I can't help but be impressed by it as well, even though I know how much it's costing my father to privately charter this thing. No one really believes me when I tell them my father and I haven't been spoiling ourselves with fancy vacations, multiple homes, foreign cars in every color, or anything else that people with more money than they know what to do with seem to do. Sure, my father has a ten thousand square foot apartment in New York's Upper East Side, but it's the one and only big thing he's ever splurged on since my mom died and he sold his first app. For sixteen years we lived comfortably, but modestly, and didn't spend money on unnecessary or extravagant things.

And then he met Allyson at a charity event a year ago. As much as I can't stand the woman and her equally money-hungry daughter, I would never blame all of his current money problems on her if the accusations were unfounded. But I refuse to believe it's a coincidence that my father's wealth started to quickly disappear exactly a year ago, which has led to unpaid personal bills, unpaid business bills, and unpaid taxes, which has led to the IRS practically living at his office building, going over every piece of paper with a fine tooth comb.

Even though I don't make an obscene amount of money working for my father, and what I do make wouldn't even cover one percent of one tax bill, I still met with the head of payroll a month ago when my father was out of town on business. I told them I needed to stop drawing a salary for the time being. Even if my father wants to turn a blind eye to all of his problems, I can't. I won't let him lose the company he built from the ground up, out of the basement of the two-bedroom cottage he purchased with my mom after they first got married, where they would lie in bed at night dreaming about all the things they would buy when they weren't living paycheck-to-paycheck, struggling to make ends meet.

Two crew members from the yacht walk across the gangway that connects it to the dock. My father introduces everyone to them, and one of them leads the way on board while the other one gets busy grabbing our luggage from the multiple carts my father had to pay a few locals to push down the dock since my evil stepsister and stepmonster couldn't possibly condense their things into one suitcase, or leave any of the purchases they made back at the hotel since, *"Have you seen the type of people who work here? You know they'd rob us blind the first chance they got."*

"Dibs on the one with the blond hair named Ben. You can have Eddie with the dark hair since I know you're a sucker for men with dark hair," Brooke whispers, winking at Eddie when we walk past him, causing him to blush a deep shade of red and drop one of the suitcases.

"That is a Louis Vuitton, limited edition, vintage trunk!" Arianna shouts, stopping halfway across the gangway to glare at Eddie. "If you scuff it, it's coming out of your salary! Daddy, tell him to be careful with my luggage!"

I cringe when I hear her call my father *daddy* and swallow back the vomit rising up in my throat. She only calls him that when she wants something, knowing it makes my father melt like butter and agree to anything she asks.

Brooke and I wait at the end of the gangway for my father to rush back, pull a hundred-dollar bill out of his pocket and hand it to Eddie with a sheepish smile while he kindly requests for Eddie to be a little more careful.

Once Arianna is mollified and we can finally continue on our way, Brooke and I pull up the rear, all of us following behind Ben single-file across the gangway until we get to the wide, outside balcony that runs along the entire length of the ship and we spread out.

Ben and my father make small talk about the weather as they lead the way to the back of the ship, Allyson and Arianna mutter complaints about how we should have chartered a bigger yacht, and Brooke whispers in my ear about Ben's fine ass and muscular arms busting out of his navy blue polo, using her hands to guesstimate the size of his penis. I can't contain my laughter when she holds her hands at least three feet apart and wags her eyebrows up and down.

The two of us are still giggling like little girls and whispering under our breaths about the state of Ben's supposed giant penis when we finally make it to the back of the ship and see the captain and the rest of the crew lined up next to him, all wearing the matching uniform of a navy blue polo on top, the guys wearing khaki shorts and the women wearing khaki skirts. As the captain introduces himself and goes down the line introducing his crew, my trailing giggles come to an abrupt halt and my jaw drops in the most unladylike fashion when he gets to the tall drink of water at the very end.

"And this our Bosun, Declan McGillis. He's in charge of…"

I don't hear another word Captain Michael says as he lists Declan's job duties on the ship. I'm too busy staring at the man, who has to be over six feet tall, with a lean build and just enough muscle definition in his arms to prove he does a lot of heavy lifting. Declan stares straight ahead as the captain continues talking and my eyes trail across the cut of his pectoral muscles that I can see perfectly with the way his polo stretches tightly across his chest. His dark brown hair is shaved close to his head on the sides and stands up in messy spikes on top. A muscle ticks at the corner of his neatly shaven jaw as the captain lists all of the things Declan is responsible for and his green eyes remain unblinking and unmoving during all of it.

I realize I'm still standing here with my mouth open when Brooke's elbow jabs me roughly in my side. I blink out of my lust-filled daze that was made even more potent when I noticed tattoos trailing down one of his arms. Yes, I'm one of those typical women who think guys are a hundred times hotter when they have tattoos. I'm a sucker for the bad boys and I'm not even ashamed to admit it.

Brooke's elbow connects with my ribs again and I finally manage to tear my eyes away from the hot guy long enough to realize everyone is staring at me. Including him. *Especially* him.

While Allyson and Ariana look at me in annoyance with their hands on their hips, my father stares at me with an embarrassed, nervous smile. Brooke is outright laughing at me, and the crew just looks at me expectantly with matching smiles glued to their faces. *He's* looking at me with one corner of his mouth tipped up in a smirk and a cocky look in his eyes.

"Mackenzie, the captain asked if you'd like to use the jet skis right after we take off, or if you'd rather relax and wait until we get to St. John tomorrow," my father says, repeating what the captain must have said when I was busy ogling the smug bastard whose face is now back to being emotionless as he stares at a spot over my shoulder. I wonder if I imagined the smirk.

"Oh, um, tomorrow is fine. I don't want you to go to any trouble. I'm sure you have a lot to do once we take off and get going," I respond quickly, smiling at the captain.

"It's no trouble at all. Declan and the rest of the crew are at your service twenty-four-seven, ready and willing to do whatever you need," he reassures me.

My eyes glance back down the line to Declan when the captain says his name and I see that muscle ticking in his jaw again. His smooth, perfectly chiseled jaw that dreams are made of.

The captain dismisses everyone in the crew aside from a woman named Ashley, and excuses himself to head up to the bridge so he can begin getting the ship ready to leave the dock. I force myself not to stare at Declan when he walks around to the balcony on the opposite side of the ship and disappears around the corner.

Ashley motions for everyone to follow her as she leads us inside and gives a tour of the guest quarters, which are nicer than any hotel I've ever seen or stayed at. When we get to the bedrooms, Ariana immediately picks the second largest one next to the master suite, while Brooke grabs my arm and stops me from continuing behind everyone.

"You've got a little drool on your chin, need me to wipe it off?" she asks in a low voice, even though Ariana is currently complaining that she can't possibly be expected to sleep in a bed with sheets that have anything less than an eight-hundred thread count. The high volume of her nasally whine drowns out every sound within a one-block radius.

"Kiss my ass, I don't have drool on my chin," I fire back, crossing my arms indignantly in front of me.

"Total bullshit, but I'll let it slide for now. I'm going to assume you'd like to swap Eddie for Declan, considering I think you might have gotten pregnant just by looking at him," she laughs.

"I'm not swapping anything or anyone. And like I told you when you suggested, multiple times, that a quick fling with a deckhand I'll never see again after we leave this boat is the best way to take my mind off of my troubles, it's not happening," I remind her. "I'm not having sex with some guy I just met that I'll be stuck on a boat with for ten days. It's bad enough I'll be stranded out in the middle of the ocean with my new family, I don't need the added misery of not being able to escape a one-night-stand."

While Arianna continues to find things to complain about and my father and Allyson get settled in the master suite, Ashley leaves us to go check on our luggage. Brooke and I make our way down the hall to the smallest bedroom, which is still three times the size of my bedroom in my apartment in Manhattan.

"I get it, you're not the one-night-stand kind of woman, but I'm just saying, there's nothing like breaking out of your comfort zone, especially with that gorgeous specimen who couldn't take his eyes off of you," Brooke tells me as I poke my head into the bathroom before taking in the rest of the beautifully decorated room with its two king sized beds.

I don't even have time to feel guilty about all the expensive furnishings and stress over the money my father didn't bat an eye about spending because I'm too busy thinking about what Brooke just said. Even if I didn't imagine the cocky, smug look on Declan's face, the idea that he was staring at *me* just as much as I was staring at *him* is enough to set off a whole swarm of butterflies in my stomach.

As Brooke starts checking out the size of the dresser drawers and muttering a "Holy shit" when she opens the closet doors and sees how big it is, I press a hand to my stomach and remind myself that no matter how good looking the guy is, I am *not* having a fling with him or anyone else on this boat. I'll suffer through the next ten days with a fake smile on my face for my father's benefit, but there is no way I'm making things even more uncomfortable on this family vacation by screwing someone on the crew…no matter how lickable his jaw is or how much my fingers are still itching to trace over every inch of the tattoo on his muscular arm.

No having sex on the boat. Period. End of story.

CHAPTER 3

Declan

"IT'S TOO HOT, the closets are too small, the color scheme is hideous, you really expect me to go barefoot for ten days just so I don't scuff these second-rate floors?" Ben whines in a high-pitched voice, mimicking the two annoying blondes that boarded the yacht a few hours ago.

"Can you believe that older bitch actually asked for orange juice with pulp in her mimosa, took a sip, then handed it back to me and demanded I strain out all the pulp?" Zoe complains as she helps us drain and scrub the Jacuzzi on the sundeck after the daughter of the "older bitch" said she saw a hair floating in the water and wouldn't go anywhere near it until we fixed the problem.

Normally, Zoe wouldn't help with anything on the exterior of the boat since she's a stew, but Ashley felt bad about the abuse she'd had to endure after serving the women lunch and told Zoe to take a fifteen-minute break. Zoe quickly ran outside and found Ben and me up on the sundeck, choosing to help us during her break instead of spending time inside, in close proximity to the guests who could run into her and bark more orders at her.

While Ben and Zoe traded horror stories about the blondes, who had already managed to piss off every member of the crew in the short time they'd been on board, I kept my head down and my mouth shut as I scrubbed the inside of the Jacuzzi so hard my muscles started screaming in protest. Since I'd been busy helping the captain lift the anchor and performing all of my duties required for us to leave the dock, I'd managed to avoid the twins of terror and all their complaining. Listening to all of the shit Ben and Zoe dealt with or overheard happen was enough to piss me off, but not the main reason I almost scrubbed the color off the walls of the Jacuzzi as I took my anger out on the huge tub.

My irritation at the moment lies all at the feet of one Mackenzie Armstrong. No, she didn't snap orders at any of the stews, and no, she didn't complain about one damn thing. She did whatever she could to *not* ask anyone for anything and, when she had to, she almost looked embarrassed that she had to ask someone to do something for her. And she never forgot her manners, always saying please and thank you, and following each one up with a wide, genuine smile. A gorgeous smile that made her ocean blue eyes sparkle on a face with smooth, sun-kissed skin. A head full of thick, shiny hair the same color as the mahogany wood accents in the guest quarters, which fell down around her shoulders in long waves, attached to a slim body with curves in all the right places accented by a short and tight tattered jean skirt, and a generous helping of cleavage that peeked out of the edge of her low-cut tank top that I could immediately tell was not attached to fake tits of any kind. They were perfect and they were real and every time she leaned over the table on the main deck during lunch, I couldn't stop staring at them when I was supposed to be wiping off the wet footprints on the deck that Arianna tracked all the way back there after her quick dip in the Jacuzzi.

The same Jacuzzi we had to fucking drain and clean when she saw a hair that was probably a strand from the fake-ass extensions on her own damn head.

Not helping matters at the moment is the fact that I can't stop thinking about the way I caught Mackenzie staring at me when she was supposed to be listening to the rules on the ship and safety instructions. It doesn't matter what kind of guy you are or what sort of moral code you hold yourself to, when a woman as hot as Mackenzie Armstrong is staring at you like she's trying to picture you naked, it's impossible to put it out of your mind.

The way her eyes were glazed over, the way her tongue darted out and slowly licked her bottom lip, the way her chest pushed her tits up and out when she took a few rapid breaths…

"What's the story with that Mackenzie chick?" Ben asks, my ears perking up at just the sound of her name, pissing me off all over again as I scrub the Jacuzzi with more gusto. "She's the only brunette in a sea of blondes and she's actually nice. Is she even related to those assholes?"

Since Ben wasn't included in the dossier meeting yesterday, and I only gave him and Eddie the basics on the guests, he doesn't know Mackenzie isn't related to the two blonde she-devils. I'm assuming since her father is also blond, she must have gotten her dark hair from her mother, wherever she is.

Since Ashley was more forthcoming with *her* crew on the Armstrong family details, Zoe takes it upon herself to explain the family dynamic to Ben.

"I overheard Mackenzie and her friend, Brooke, talking and I guess Mackenzie's mom died when she was little. Her dad never dated anyone until Miss Resting Bitch face came along and brought RBF Junior with her," Zoe tells him.

My frantic scrubbing comes to a stop when she says this, making me realize Mackenzie and I have something in common. We both lost parents at a young age. Too bad that's where the similarities end and I resume my washing with an irritated grunt. It doesn't matter that we've both experienced loss, her with her mother and me with both of my parents, she's still so far out of my league it's not even funny. And it's more than a little pathetic that I'm thinking about this considering she's a guest and she's off limits, no matter how gorgeous or seemingly unlike the rest of her family she is.

"She's being nice now, but just give it a day or two. She'll be looking down her nose at you and putting you in your place, I guarantee it. They're all the same, even if they want to pretend like they aren't. Rich, entitled assholes who think they're better than you," I mutter, leaning up out of the Jacuzzi and rolling the kinks out of my shoulders.

"I don't know; she seems really different. And her friend, Brooke, is nice too," Zoe muses, putting the hose into the tub and turning on the water to begin filling it again. "The dad isn't so bad when you get him away from the wife and the stepdaughter. I kind of feel bad for him. He follows them around like a little puppy and agrees with whatever they say, but when they aren't around, he's sweet and charming."

"Awwwww, does Zoe have a crush on the old rich dude?" Ben jokes.

She throws her towel at his face and shakes her head at him.

"Sorry, old dudes aren't my type, no matter how much money they have. Also, dudes, period, aren't my type. Remember Benny-boy?"

Zoe is a lesbian and it's probably one of the main reasons we get along so well. She doesn't have to worry about me doing something stupid like trying to get in her pants, and I don't have to worry about having a drunken hookup with her and her turning into a psycho.

"Fine. I'll take one for the team and snag me a rich bitch if you two are going to pass," Ben says, leaning against the deck railing with a smile.

"Stay the fuck away from Mackenzie. She's off limits," I growl, the words coming out of my mouth before I can stop them.

Ben and Zoe both stare at me with equal looks of shock on their face for a few seconds before Ben tosses his head back and howls with laughter.

"Holy shit, you already broke your own cardinal rule and have a crush on one of the guests!" he exclaims through his laughs. "And only a few hours after you met the chick. That's got to be some kind of a record."

His full-blown laughter dies down to a few chuckles when I glare at him, and Zoe covers her mouth with her hand to hide her own amused smile.

"I don't have a crush on Mackenzie, get your head out of your ass."

The lie flies right off my tongue as visions of Mackenzie's tits and ass and long smooth legs float through my mind, and I start wondering what all that long thick hair would feel like brushing against my thighs while she wrapped those full pink lips around my cock.

"She's off limits because she's a guest. Period," I add, shifting my feet and stealthily rearranging the painful hard-on in my shorts behind the cover of the back wall of the Jacuzzi.

"Sorry, man, I didn't sign any contract when I started working on this ship that guests were off limits, and neither did you. There's no rule that says we can't have a little fun to break up the monotony of being a slave to the rich and famous," Ben informs me.

While we didn't sign any damn contracts, it's still an unwritten rule in yachting. One that if broken, could result in serious consequences. Ben might not care about getting mixed up with a guest and, when things go sour, she complains to the captain and he loses his job, but I do. I can't lose this job. Even though we make shit money on an hourly basis, the tips we get at the end of a charter more than make up for that as long as the guests aren't total douchebags and give us the standard ten to twenty percent of the charter fee. With this charter, especially, one of the longest and most expensive ones we have booked for the season, costing Mark Armstrong $200,000, that can equal a tip up to twenty grand. With me and my two deckhands, Ashley and her two stews splitting that baby equally six ways means we each take home around $3,300 cash under the table. For ten days of work.

I won't do anything to jeopardize that tip, this job,

or my plans for the future. I need to keep racking up the yachting hours so I can sit for my captain's exam. I need the money to send home to my baby sister, and I need to save everything that's left over so I can captain my own boat one day. A pair of tits and a great ass, no matter how spectacular they are, will *not* distract me.

I open my mouth to remind Ben of all of this, when he pushes off the railing, comes around to the back of the Jacuzzi and smacks his hand down on my shoulder.

"Don't worry, I won't poach your territory. Mackenzie isn't really my type anyway," Ben tells me with a wink. "She's hot and all, but I've got my sights set on that Brooke chick. I saw her staring down the blonde bitches when they got shitty with your girl. She got a crazy look in her eyes, like she could reach across the table and stab them and not lose any sleep over it. You know I've got a thing for the crazy ones."

Ben gives me another pat on the shoulder before sticking his hands in his pockets.

"Although, if you want to make any headway with your girl, you're going to have to do a little more than grunt and snarl and stare at her tits all the time like you did when you were introduced to her. I'd suggest talking. I've heard the ladies like a good chat every now and again."

With that, he turns and walks away, whistling as he goes.

"SHE'S NOT MY GIRL!" I shout back lamely,

unable to come up with any other kind of comeback.

Zoe laughs, and I aim my irritation with this entire situation at her.

"Anything you'd like to add?" I fire at her.

She shakes her head, fighting hard to hide the smile on her face.

"Nope," Zoe replies, popping the "p" at the end.

There are a few minutes of comfortable silence between us as we both look out over the railing at the setting sun as we make our way to St. John. Right when I start to relax and forget about the stupid shit that came out of Ben's mouth, Zoe changes her mind about having anything to add.

"My break's over, so I better get back inside and start getting everything ready for dinner," she says, moving around the tub and towards the sliding glass doors that lead into the formal dining room. "But if you decide to stop grunting and staring at Mackenzie's tits anytime soon, I can help you come up with some excellent conversation starters. I'm pretty good at chatting up the ladies and getting in their pants."

Without turning around, I lift my arm in the air and give her the finger, her laughter fading with the slide of the doors as she goes inside.

I drop my arm back down to my side and stare into the Jacuzzi as it fills. As soon as I'm finished with this, I have to head around to the main deck aft where the outside dining table is set up for guests to eat when we don't have high winds or bad weather, to help the stews with bartending duties while they're busy serving dinner.

I do everything I can to clear my mind of perfect tits, a great ass and hair brushing against my thighs while I shut off the water, wind up the hose and stick it back into the small storage closet. Having a fucking hard-on in front of the guests is probably frowned upon.

I just need to get my head back in the game, focus on doing my job and forget about everything else. I've done it a thousand times before and I'm not going to let Mackenzie Armstrong fuck with my head or my dick, no matter how *nice* and *different* she's pretending to be. She'll show her true colors, it's only a matter of time. I can keep my dick in check until then, no problem.

CHAPTER 4

⚓

Mackenzie

"REMEMBER THAT LITTLE diner we went to in Pennsylvania? You were what, eleven?" my dad asks, leaning back in his chair and sipping his after-dinner coffee.

"Twelve," I reply with a smile as my dad returns it, and his eyes soften with the memory. "It was called Mom's Open Kitchen and they had—"

"The best french fries in the world!" my dad finishes, and we both laugh.

I'm not even going to lie; dinner was the most uncomfortable moment so far on this trip. The food was amazing, sitting on the upper deck watching the sun set over the ocean as we slowly made our way to St. John was a beautiful experience, but the company left a lot to be desired. Allyson and Arianna complained about every dish that was served and sent it back to the kitchen, bitched at the crew when they weren't fast enough, and never once thanked them for anything. It was embarrassing and I lost count of how many times I apologized for their behavior to the crew, under my breath so the two hellions wouldn't hear and have one more thing to bitch about.

Even more embarrassing was the fact that Declan stood at the small bar a few feet away from our table and had to listen to this shit all night long. And deal with their nonsense as well since, according to them, every drink he made tasted like the bottom of a shoe. I don't know why it bothers me so much more to have him witness my family's behavior. I don't even know the guy. I shouldn't care what he thinks of me or the people I'm related to by marriage. Having one of the hottest guys I've ever laid eyes on see how they act somehow makes it a thousand times more humiliating, and makes me hope he's not thinking I'm *anything* like them. Every time one of them screeched out another complaint or order, my eyes would automatically glance in his direction, hoping he hadn't heard it, and I'd catch him looking at me. It made my heart beat faster and my palms sweat and my skin heat up in a way the hot tropical sun could never do. It made me forget, for just a moment, that I was on a vacation with two people I couldn't stand, on a yacht we couldn't afford to charter, with a father who barely noticed me since these women came into his life and turned it upside down.

At least with a full belly and the two women in question busy taking selfies at the end of the table, he seemed to be able to relax for a few minutes and I could easily pretend Allyson and Arianna weren't even there and it was just the two of us. Like it used to be.

"What was the name of the place that had a giant stuffed grizzly bear and you could sit on its lap and take a picture?" dad asks, leaning forward to rest his elbows on the table and hold his coffee cup between his two hands.

"That was—"

"BORING!" Allyson shouts, cutting me off as she gets up from the table and walks down to stand behind my father, draping her arms around his shoulders. "God, you two and your stupid, old stories. How many times do we have to hear them? They're putting me to sleep."

Brooke reaches over from her chair next to me, grabs my hand and gives it a squeeze. With my free hand, I snatch the full glass of wine in front of me and chug it until it's gone, slamming it back down on the table a little roughly.

"I'm so sorry, honey," my dad apologizes to Allyson, setting his cup down on the table and reaching up to pat her arm.

Our trip down memory lane is quickly forgotten as he looks up at her with a beaming smile, and I try not to throw up in my mouth when she tells him she's ready for bed, and that she bought some new lingerie for him to unwrap.

Dad pushes back from the table and gives Brooke, Arianna, and myself a kiss on the cheek, bidding us goodnight before he grabs Allyson's hand and pulls her through the sliding glass doors.

"Well, that was enough to make all that delicious food we ate come right back up," Brooke mutters, letting go of my hand to take her own huge drink of wine.

"Do my boobs look perky enough? I was thinking of getting them lifted." Arianna announces at the other end of the table to no one in particular, her hands cupping the boobs in question that my father already paid a hefty price to get enlarged two months ago.

"Never mind. THAT'S enough to make me vomit," Brooke adds with a grimace.

We both watch in silent disgust as Arianna pushes her boobs together and up, before Brooke shakes her head and turns away to look at me.

"You really need to have a heart-to-heart with your father. I thought this vacation would be good for you and a way to relax from all the stress, but I can still see it all over your face," she informs me. "And I've seen you checking emails on your phone a hundred times since we boarded this ship. I thought we agreed when we got to St. Thomas that you would forget about work."

I sigh, twisting my empty wine glass around by the

stem.

"I can't just forget about it, Brooke. I've got accountants and lawyers asking me a hundred different questions all day long. Our problems aren't going away just because I'm out of town."

"Do you even hear yourself?" she asks with a raise of her eyebrows. "*Our* problems. They aren't *our* problems, they're your father's problems. That he's chosen to ignore. You can't clean up all his messes, Mackenzie. You need to live your own life and let him deal with the consequences of his mistakes."

I open my mouth to argue and she holds her hand up to silence me.

"I know; I get it. It was just the two of you for a really long time and you're not the kind of person who can sit back and watch her father fail," she continues. "But, hon, you can't go down with him. You gave up everything for him after college when he begged you not to move away, and you're *still* doing it. You're still sacrificing your happiness for him. You've been working yourself to the bone for six months, ever since the first subpoena was delivered to his office. You don't eat, you don't sleep, you take work home every night and you forgot how to live. I can't sit back and watch you do this to yourself anymore. You need to sit him down and talk to him, or I will."

Everything Brooke says to me is true, yet every word she says breaks my heart into a million pieces. I *did* give up my dreams after college for my father. I *did* stop living six months ago when his company started falling apart at the seams. And he hasn't even noticed or cared.

"Alright, that's enough heart-to-heart for one evening," she declares, lifting her wine glass to her lips and finishing off the rest of it. "I've been watching Mr. Hottie Pants over there stare at you all night when you weren't looking and, sweet mother of God, the looks he's been giving you were enough to make *me* have an orgasm. Get over there and get yourself some."

The tears that had been prickling the back of my eyes just seconds ago immediately disappear, and I let out a quiet laugh. I subtly glance back over my shoulder, pretending like I'm looking out at the ocean, even though it's pitch black and I can't see anything. Declan has his head down and is busy washing drink glasses in the sink attached to the bar. Instead of the navy blue polo he had on earlier, tonight all of the crew changed into white polos. The white cotton material brings out the tanned skin of his muscular arms and, once again, I'm stuck in a lust-filled daze staring at the full-sleeve tattoo on his arm, wanting to run my hand over it and feel his muscles tighten under my fingers.

Maybe Brooke is right. I just need to relax and have some fun. I'm not the kind of woman to have a one-night-stand, though. Maybe some harmless flirting is just what I need to forget about the stress of the last six months and remember what it's like to have some fun and live a little.

"I think maybe I'll go get another glass of wine," I muse, turning my head back around to wink at Brooke and grab my empty glass from the table.

Her entire face lights up with a huge smile as I push my chair back and smooth the skirt of my sundress down with my free hand.

"Go get 'em, tiger!" she whispers, slapping my ass when I turn away from the table, making me let out a little yelp. "And find out where that other hot guy, Ben, disappeared to!"

I shoot her a dirty look over my shoulder and she just grins at me.

Declan is still busy washing glasses and doesn't notice me walking up to the bar, so I move around to the back and reach for the bottle of Pinot Grigio he uncorked for me earlier that's still sitting on top. As soon as my hand wraps around the neck of the bottle, it's quickly snatched away from me.

"What are you doing?" Declan asks in a low voice, so close to my ear that I realize he's standing right next to me. I can feel the heat from his body right through the thin material of my sundress.

"I, uh...getting more wine?" I ask in confusion, holding up my empty glass between us, pretending like the close proximity of his body to mine isn't affecting me in the least.

He stares down at me with a frown, and all I can do

is focus on his lips and wonder what they'd feel like against my skin. He smells like soap and a subtle hint of spicy cologne, making my mouth so dry that I have to wet my lips with my tongue. His eyes flash down to the movement of my tongue swiping across my bottom lip and I watch the green orbs darken, making me want to roar with the newfound feminine power I didn't even know I had.

"It's not your job to pour your own wine, princess."

Even though the rough, gravelly sound of his voice makes me tingle in all the right places, his words quickly douse the fire and make me take a step back from him in irritation.

He grabs the empty wine glass out of my hand and sets it on top of the bar, turning his body away from me to refill it. Without looking at me, he slides the glass across the bar top and gives me his back as he recorks the bottle and sets it aside.

His words sting in a way that never has from anyone else before and it pisses me off. I know I've had a privileged life that most people dream of. I know from the outside looking in, it seems like we have it all and don't have a care in the world. But I've never taken anything for granted. I've never acted like a *princess* or gotten something that I didn't work my ass off for. And this man, who doesn't even know me, has no right to judge me.

Angrily grabbing the glass, I tip it back and down

the entire thing, wishing I had the balls to tell him to go to hell. Too bad he's still the hottest damn guy I've ever seen, and even his poor judgment isn't enough to make me completely immune to him. I've never been one to shy away from a challenge, and Declan McGillis just moved to the top of my to-do-list.

That thought makes a little giggle bubble up and out of my mouth and I realize I might have had a little too much wine, a little too quickly, and it's pathetic I'm such a lightweight.

"Uuuugghhh I'm so BORED. Hey, waiter! I need a refill over here!" Arianna shouts from the table, holding her empty glass up in the air and shaking it, making the ice cubes tinkle against the glass.

My anger with Declan quickly dissipates when I hear him sigh. No wonder he was so quick to judge me. Look at the people I'm surrounded by.

"Declan!" I yell over to Arianna as I see him start to make her another drink out of the corner of my eye.

"What?" she replies in irritation, her eyes narrowing as they stare me down.

"Dec-lan," I repeat, sounding out his name slowly. "His name is Declan, not *waiter*."

She rolls her eyes and slams her glass down on the table. "Jeez, mega-bitch much?"

"Jeez, mega-stick-up-your-ass much?" I fire back, which earns me a wide-eyed, jaw-dropping laugh from Brooke when she turns around to give me a thumbs up.

45

My cheeks heat with embarrassment that I stooped to Arianna's level. I never engage in a verbal smack-down with her because it's pointless, and I refuse to play her childish games. When I hear a soft chuckle come from Declan, my head whips in his direction and I suddenly feel better about sticking up for myself. He quickly wipes the amused smile from his face and clears his throat, turning back to finish slicing a lime for Arianna's vodka and soda.

Brooke has been trying to get me to tell Arianna off for a year and I've never had the balls to do it. Some liquid courage and the knowledge that Declan was standing right here witnessing how my stepsister treats me suddenly gave me some much needed bravery. I didn't want him to think I let Arianna walk all over me, even if it were true. For some reason I can't explain, I didn't want Declan to think I was weak.

Arianna shoots daggers at me for all of three seconds, and then pulls out her cell phone and starts taking stupid, duck-face selfies.

"You wouldn't happen to have an ice pick back there, would you?" I ask Declan, holding my glass out to him when I see he already has the cork back off the bottle anticipating my need for a refill.

"Yeah, why?" he replies, emptying the bottle into my glass before chucking it into a garbage can under the bar.

"I'd like to stab her in the back of the skull with it,"

I tell him casually as I bring the glass up to my mouth.

He doesn't hide his amusement this time, his quiet laugh tipping the corners of his mouth up into a smile that makes the dimples pop out in his cheeks.

Shit. Dimples. I'm definitely having a quick fling with this guy. No woman can resist dimples.

I move out from around the bar before I do something stupid, like lean in and lick his dimples right in front of Brooke and my evil stepsister.

He watches me go without saying a word. His piercing stare starts up that damn swarm of butterflies in my stomach all over again, as well as a tingling between my legs that makes walking back to my seat without rubbing my thighs together less than easy. I lift up my glass of wine to toast him as I walk backwards to the table.

"Thanks for the wine, Deck. Keep that ice pick handy for me, would ya?"

He grins at me before I turn around and take my seat next to Brooke.

"Soooooo, tell me everything. I tried to hear what was going on, but Malibu Barbie over there wouldn't shut up about her tits while you were gone," Brooke complains, pointing her thumb over her shoulder in Arianna's direction, who is still holding her phone above her head trying to get the perfect angle for a selfie. "Also, nice work shutting her up. I didn't think you had it in you."

With a big grin, I take a deep breath and blurt out a

reply before I lose my nerve.

"I think I'm gonna need some pointers on how to have a vacation fling."

Brooke lets out a loud *whoop* and I quickly smack my hand against her mouth while I laugh at her excitement, realizing this is the first time in months I've actually smiled and have been excited about something.

Declan McGillis just might be the cure to all my problems.

CHAPTER 5

⚓

Declan

AFTER CLEANING UP the bar area and grabbing Eddie to do our nightly check, making sure everything on the exterior is secure—all pillows and cushions put away, lounge chairs folded up, Jacuzzi covered, and pick up any other messes the guests have made—I check my watch and realize it's after one in the morning. I'm exhausted, I'm irritated, and all I want to do is go to bed and try to forget about the woman who made me laugh tonight.

Grabbing the glassware and leftover liquor from where I left it on a tray on the bar, I head inside the ship and through the main salon, wanting nothing more than to fall into my tiny bunk, close my eyes and will away the fucking hard-on I've had since Mackenzie told that bitch off when she called me *waiter*. Never, in all my thirty-two years, has the sound of my own name out of a woman's mouth ever made me this hard. I've never liked nicknames, but just hearing the soft way she called me *Deck* when she lifted her wine glass in a toast, and how she made me smile all over again when she brought up the ice pick, made me want to round the bar, yank her against me and see if her lips were as soft as they looked.

I've lost my Goddamn mind over a woman I just met and I don't like it. As I head down the narrow stairs to the galley, the sound of pots and pans clanging to the floor make me groan, realizing I'm going to have to deal with Marcel and his fucking attitude before I can even think of trying to get Mackenzie Armstrong and the way she said my name out of my head.

Walking through the steward's pantry, I set the tray of glasses and extra bottles of alcohol down on the counter next to the sink, cursing to myself when I hear another loud crash of pans hit the floor.

"Marcel, you really need to calm your shit. I know the guests were assholes tonight, but—"

I stop short when I get to the doorway of the galley and realize it wasn't Marcel making all that noise in here. Ben stands in the middle of a pile of pots and pans, his body in between the thighs of a woman he's currently got perched up on the counter in front of him. Ben is looking at me over his shoulder with a big grin on his face that doesn't show an ounce of embarrassment at being caught, and the woman lifts one arm from around his shoulders to give me a wave, not even bothering to unwrap her legs from around Ben's waist.

"Declan, Brooke, Brooke, Declan," Ben introduces easily, his hands still resting on the woman's bare thighs where he pushed the skirt of her dress up during their make-out session.

"I know who she is," I reply, gritting my teeth, wondering why in the hell I have a best friend who doesn't know the first thing about following rules.

This morning he was fucking a stew, and tonight he's well on his way to fucking a guest. And not just any guest, the best friend of Mackenzie. One look at this woman, with her face flushed and her hair all disheveled, and I'm right back to thinking about *her*. Wondering if *her* mouth would be red and swollen after I tasted her, wondering if the skin of *her* chest would flush with desire when I touched her, wondering how my name would sound if she moaned it...

"Sorry, I know I'm not supposed to be down here, but I couldn't help myself. I had to come looking for this guy," Brooke informs me, her body still wrapped around Ben, neither one of them making any move to leave the galley.

"Glad you found me, baby," Ben tells her with a wink, making me roll my eyes. "Hey, didn't you say your friend couldn't sleep and that's why you came looking for me?"

Ben looks back over his shoulder at me and gives

me a lecherous smile that makes me want to pick up one of the pans from the floor by his feet and smack him over the fucking head with it.

"Why yes, yes I did," Brooke replies casually. "Mackenzie decided to go for a walk around the deck, and I got bored in that room all by myself. Last time I checked, she was on the right side."

That's called starboard, baby," Ben tells her, turning away from me to run his hands up her thighs until he's clutching her ass.

"It's so hot when you talk boat," Brooke replies. "Tell me more."

"Port, starboard, stern, bridge…"

Brooke tightens her arms around Ben's shoulders, giving him encouraging moans when he dips his head and mutters more nautical terms against the skin of her throat.

Thoroughly disgusted with what is happening right in front of me, and hoping to God Brooke isn't a vindictive woman who will lose her shit when she finds out the kind of man-whore Ben is, I turn away from them to get the hell out of here.

"Hey, Declan!" Brooke calls to me suddenly. "Can you do me a HUGE favor and go make sure Mackenzie gets back to our room okay? This is a pretty big ship and I don't want her getting lost or anything."

With my back still to them, I sigh and give a little wave over my shoulder, my feet moving me back through the stew pantry at a clipped pace when I start hearing giggles and moans coming from the galley.

Instead of heading right to my bunk like I know I should, my legs take me in the opposite direction and back up the stairs to the guest quarters. I tell myself the entire way I am absolutely *not* going in search of Mackenzie. She got a tour of the ship just like everyone else, and if she gets lost, it's her own damn fault. I'm going upstairs to do one last check and make sure Eddie and I didn't miss anything, that's it.

I take my time looking around the stern, jiggling all the cabinet doors to make sure they're all secure and nothing will fall out of them overnight. By the time I finish and make my way to the starboard side of the ship, I'm positive I've wasted enough time and Mackenzie will have found her way back to her room. When I get halfway down the length of the ship, checking the deck for anything that shouldn't be there, I sense her before I even see her. My feet stop moving and my head slowly comes up to find her standing against the railing, looking out at the water.

She's still wearing the same light blue strapless dress she had on at dinner. With the full moon shining brightly overhead, I see the light ocean breeze moving strands of her long, dark hair around her face and gently rustling the short skirt around her thighs, lifting it up until I can see so much of one smooth upper thigh that my mouth waters to run my hands over it.

My heart thumps wildly in my chest as I stand here staring at her looking so beautiful in the moonlight that it takes my breath away. I should turn around, walk back inside, go to my bunk and forget I ever saw her.

I know that's what I *should* do, but it's not what I want to do and it pisses me off. I can still hear her saying my name earlier. When something makes her turn her head in my direction, the surprised look on her face turns into a slow smile, and all of the blood in my body shoots right to my dick. My feet that felt like cement blocks stuck to the deck floor just seconds ago start moving me towards her. When she sees me coming, she turns her body to face me fully, one hand clutching a handful of her hair to stop it from blowing in her face, and the other holding tightly to the railing. I move faster, stalking towards her until I see her eyes widen in shock.

I can't return her smile, I can't say a word, all I can do is charge her like an animal, my hands clenched into fists at my sides and my dick so painfully hard in my shorts all I can think about is getting some fucking relief.

She opens her mouth when I'm a foot away.

"What are you—"

I close the distance in record time, grab her face with my hands, bend my knees, dip my head and claim those full, gorgeous pink lips. Her mouth immediately opens for me, gasping, and I take the opportunity to dart my tongue inside. As soon as it touches hers, a shock of need shoots right through my body. I try to control myself, but when the shock leaves her and she immediately swirls her tongue around mine, kissing me back and moaning into my mouth, I'm done for.

My hands drop from her face and I wrap my arms around her waist, yanking her roughly against my body as we both battle to deepen the kiss. Our tongues push and pull against each other, our heads tilt from side to side to get the best angle, and before I know it, I'm turning her around and pushing her roughly into the wall of the ship.

Her hands fist into my hair and clench tightly as I bend my knees and push myself between her thighs. She moans into my mouth again when I push up, and slide my aching cock against her as she lifts one leg and hooks it around the back of mine, pulling me tightly to her. I kiss her harder, deeper, with more urgency than I've ever felt with any other woman. My hips thrust against her in the same rhythm as my tongue pushing in and out of her mouth, and I feel like a fucking fifteen-year-old who could come in his pants at any second.

The heat between her thighs as she moves her own hips and rubs herself against me makes me want to pull my head back and roar. I take a second to run my tongue over her full bottom lip before diving back into her warm, wet mouth and claiming it. She sucks my tongue deeper into her mouth, and now it's my turn to groan with need, wanting more…wanting *everything* from this woman. She smells like coconuts from the suntan lotion she put on earlier; she tastes like the sweet wine she drank at dinner…

The dinner my crew served her. The dinner where I was the bartender and she was the guest. The Goddamn guest that I shouldn't be mauling against the side of the fucking ship.

With every ounce of willpower I possess, I yank my mouth away from hers and take a stumbling step back from her body. Her leg drops from around mine and her hands drop from their hold on my hair. I continue moving backwards until I smack into the deck railing, my eyes never leaving her as I watch the flushed skin of her chest rise and fall with rapid breaths. With the moonlight still shining high above us, I no longer have to wonder how her lips would look if I kissed her. I silently watch her bring one of her hands up and trail the tips of her fingers over her red, swollen lips as she stares back at me in shocked wonderment.

I want to move back to her and finish what I start-ed. Take whatever she wants to give me, reach up under her skirt, yank her panties to the side, and slam myself inside of her to ease the ache in my cock, but I can't. I shouldn't have come out here. I shouldn't have kissed her, and I sure as hell can't fuck her.

She's a guest and I'm the crew. She's out of my league and this was a mistake. At least now I don't have to wonder what she tastes like. The feel of her tongue in my mouth, the moans she made at the back of her throat, and the way her body felt molded to mine will be burned into my brain for the rest of this Goddamn trip. I'll be a professional and do my job and pretend like this moment of temporary insanity never happened.

Without a word, I turn and stalk away from her, pissed at myself for losing control with a guest. One taste, that's all I needed. Now that I've had it, now that my curiosity has been sated, I can focus on my job and forget about Mackenzie Armstrong and the best damn kiss I've had in a long time.

CHAPTER 6

⚓

Mackenzie

I T'S PAINFULLY OBVIOUS that Declan is avoiding me after what happened on the deck late last night. When Brooke left our room in search of Ben, I couldn't stop thinking about Declan and if I'd have the courage to make a move on him, so I went for a walk to try to clear my head so I could sleep. I never imagined as I stood staring out at the ocean that *he'd* come to *me*. The look on his face when I saw him standing there watching me was clear he wasn't happy about finding me out there alone, and I was more than a little surprised when he suddenly stalked towards me without saying a word. The shock continued when he grabbed my face and kissed me, but it was quickly replaced by desire.

Holy shit could that man kiss. I've never been kissed like that before, so hard and raw and brutal. I should have been embarrassed by how quickly I responded to him, how needy I must have seemed as I rubbed myself against him and couldn't stop moaning into his mouth every time his tongue swirled around mine. When I felt how hard he was for me as he pushed himself between my thighs, I forgot all about being embarrassed since it was obvious he was just as affected as I was.

Right when I'd gathered up the courage to beg him to take me up against that damn wall, he pulled away and stood there staring at me, his face a wash of irritation and regret before he turned and walked away without a word.

"Declan, Declan, I need some help setting up the water slide for the guests."

Glancing over at Ben as he holds his radio up to his mouth, I hold my breath waiting for the sound of Declan's voice over the radio. The yacht made it to St. John in the middle of the night but since they don't have a dock big enough for us, we're anchored a few miles offshore. Everyone decided to spend the day relaxing in the sun until later tonight, where the crew will take us over to the island in jetties to do some sightseeing after dinner.

All day long, Arianna and Allyson have demanded one thing or another from the crew to keep them occupied instead of just laying back in their deck chairs and enjoying the Caribbean sun like Brooke and my dad and myself.

They had them set up a huge, portable boatside swimming pool that has a mesh barrier so they can go in the water without worrying about jellyfish or other marine life bothering them. It took the crew over an hour to set up the pool and the two women spent all of five minutes in the water before they declared it was too cold.

After that, they wanted the huge water trampoline set up, which again took over an hour, and *again,* occupied them for a handful of minutes before they complained that it was boring.

So on and so forth, the crew has been running around all day to do their bidding, and each time Ben calls for Declan over the radio, Declan comes back to say he's busy with something else and to call for Eddie. Of course, this has made Brooke's day a brighter one since she told me they made out in the kitchen for over an hour last night and it was, and I quote, "mind blowing." Not only have I had to deal with two bitchy and bored women all day, I've had to listen to Brooke flirt shamelessly with Ben and watch him return it with equal fervor as he blatantly stares at her bikini-clad body and winks at her every time he walks by her chair.

It's not like I want Declan to come out here and tell me it was the best kiss he'd ever had or anything stupid like that, but a freaking "hello" would be nice after what occurred between us last night.

"Copy that," Declan's voice suddenly crackles over

Ben's radio, making my heart beat faster when I hear it. "Busy with the captain right now. Zoe's finished with lunch clean-up, so I'll send her down with Eddie to help you guys."

I try to hide my disappointment when Declan, yet again, gives an excuse to Ben about why he can't come up here to the sun deck, but it's impossible. Sighing loudly, I flop my head back against my chair and pull my sunglasses down from the top of my head to cover my eyes. I get that he's busy and he's working, but it's become glaringly obvious that he's doing whatever he can to *not* come up here, where he knows I've been since I woke up this morning, and Ben proves my theory right.

"Busy with the captain my ass," Ben mutters from the other side of Brooke's chair as he clips the radio to his belt and then looks down at her with his hands on his hips. "What the hell did your girl do to my boy last night that he won't come anywhere near her? Did she bite him? I thought he liked it rough, but maybe not."

Brooke leans over and smacks Ben's thigh with a familiarity and ease that shocks me as the two of them stare at each other and then start laughing.

"For your information, *your boy* took advantage of *my girl* last night and then left her high and dry," Brooke informs him, making me instantly regret telling her what happened when we were both in bed last night, under the covers and with the lights turned off, the darkness in the room giving me the courage to blurt it all out to her.

"Jesus, really, Brooke? And hello? I'm sitting right here. Stop talking about me," I complain, narrowing my eyes at her even though she can't see them through my dark sunglasses.

"Well, it's true. You kept me up all night with your tossing and turning. I almost threw a pillow at your head and told you to go into the bathroom and give yourself a little five-digit relief since Declan couldn't finish what he started."

Forget the hot sun above us; my embarrassment makes my face flush a thousand times worse when Ben chuckles under his breath.

"Don't worry, I'll have a talk with him."

"You will do no such thing!" I quickly tell Ben. "It was a mistake and it never should have happened. I couldn't care less where Declan is or what he's doing. I'm on vacation and I'm relaxing and I don't care about Declan. See? This is me, perfectly relaxed."

I'm rambling. I know I'm rambling as I point to myself and try to prove how relaxed I am and how much I don't care about stupid Declan McGillis and his stupid kiss, and how I tossed and turned all night because I couldn't stop rubbing my thighs together replaying that damn kiss over and over until I almost had an orgasm just thinking about it.

If he wants to avoid me, fine. No big deal. Whatever.

"Hello! We've been waiting here for like, ever! Is someone going to set up the slide for us or do we have to do it ourselves?" Allyson shouts to Ben from the other side of the sun deck.

He grumbles under his breath, gives Brooke a quick wink and then turns the biggest fake smile I've ever seen in Allyson's direction as he walks away from us and starts kissing her ass with apologies and an explanation that he's just waiting for some of the crew to come help him.

"I'm going to kill you," I mutter to Brooke when Ben is far enough away.

She just laughs as she grabs a bottle of suntan lotion from her beach bag on the deck chair next to her, sits up in her chair and starts lathering her body.

"You're forgetting I saw the dreamy, lust-filled daze in your eyes when you got back to the room last night. You can pretend not to care in front of Ben all you want, but that shit won't work on me," she explains, tossing me the bottle of Hawaiian Tropic coconut-scented lotion when she's finished with it. "He can't avoid you forever. This ship is big, but not that big. You just rest your pretty head this afternoon and let Momma Brooke come up with a plan for later."

I can't help but laugh at my friend as she relaxes back into her chair. I take my time rubbing the lotion into my skin so I don't burn. I glance over at my father who is fast asleep under his umbrella with a book resting open on his chest, ignoring my disappointment when Eddie and Zoe join Ben on the deck to help him inflate the giant slide that will hang off the edge of the boat. Part of me wants to wake my father up so he can listen to the abuse Allyson and Arianna give the crew because they aren't working fast enough to their liking, but I decide to let him be. It's not like it would matter anyway. He would just smile nervously at them and agree with whatever they said.

Tuning out the grating sounds of the two women's voices, I lay back down and work on relaxing until I need to apologize to Ben, Eddie, and Zoe when the morons go down the slide once, bitch about how boring it is and then want to do something else.

Hoping Brooke was just joking about coming up with a plan, I close my eyes and let the soothing sounds of the water lapping against the boat lull me into oblivion.

I try to tell myself that what happened last night was no big deal and it's no skin off my back if I don't see Declan again for the rest of this trip, but as I drift off to sleep, I can't stop replaying every moment of that damn kiss and what it did to my body, and I know I'm lying to myself.

CHAPTER 7

⚓

Declan

*S*UN-KISSED SKIN…*her tongue in my mouth…royal blue halter top bikini that made her tits look fantastic…those tits pressed up against my chest…the slow, torturous way she rubbed that fucking lotion all over her body…her tongue in my mouth…*

I stomp my feet angrily through the formal dining room, my thoughts battling between seeing Mackenzie in a bathing suit all day and that fucking kiss last night. Sure, I did whatever I could to not run into her, but that didn't stop me from creeping around the corner or looking down from the windows of the bridge like some kind of perverted stalker.

Jesus Christ could that woman fill out a bikini.

Ben wouldn't shut up all day about how hot Brooke looked in her red suit, but I didn't even notice anyone else out on that sundeck when I caught my first glimpse of Mackenzie after breakfast. Her olive skin got darker as the day went on, bringing out the brightness of her blue eyes whenever she'd take her sunglasses off and roll them at something her idiot family would do. Watching her stretch out those long, toned legs, point her toes and reach her arms above her head after she woke up from a nap made me want to climb on top of her body and feel the warmth from her sun-soaked skin against mine. Seeing her sit up and slowly spread lotion over her shoulders and down across her chest made me want to reach into my shorts and palm my cock while her hand rubbed against her mouth-watering cleavage.

Which is exactly what I did. After I finished watching the show and made sure Ben, Eddie, and Zoe were good setting up the slide, I ran down to the tiny bathroom attached to my bunk, locked the door behind me and jerked myself off until I came in my hand after just a few strokes, with Mackenzie's name on my lips.

Fucking woman has me tied up in knots and it needs to stop. I thought kissing her would get her out of my system, but all it's done is light a fire inside me I can't get rid of. I can't get her out of my head and I can't stop wanting her. I'm not a man-whore like Ben, but I've been with my share of women and I've even been in love once with a woman that had the same background and upbringing as Mackenzie. I don't care that I've never wanted another woman as much as Mackenzie, I've been down this road before and I know how it ends. It starts with lust, moves on to something more, and then she realizes you're not good enough for her and breaks your fucking heart. Been there, done that, bought the Goddamn t-shirt that says "You're too poor for me, and your goals aren't big enough to keep me in the lifestyle I'm accustomed to."

At least Mackenzie left with everyone else on the jetties a little bit ago to go over to the island. I won't have to worry about running into her, and with her off the ship for the rest of the night, her absence will help me forget all about her.

When I get halfway down the stairs to the galley, I hear hushed voices, the rambling of rapid-fire French words becoming louder the closer I get to the room. Preparing myself to calm down Marcel after the she-beasts once again sent back every dish he'd prepared them for dinner tonight, I come to an abrupt halt when I see Marcel isn't alone. Mackenzie is standing next to him and he has his head tossed back in laughter. He's fucking *laughing*. The man who does nothing but scowl, curse, and throw shit around the galley is standing elbow-to-elbow next to the woman who won't leave my thoughts, and she just made him laugh.

"Je ne supporte pas ces chiennes auxquelles je suis apparenté."

Marcel chuckles again when Mackenzie says something in French, and I forget all about his unusual happiness when my dick jumps to attention. So much for thinking that her saying my name last night was the hottest thing I've ever heard. This woman speaking fluently in French, even though I don't have the slightest fucking clue what she said, makes me want to drag her into the nearest bunk and make her say shit to me in French all night long while I pound into her.

Jesus Christ, what is happening to me?

Clearing my throat in irritation, Mackenzie jumps in surprise and looks over at me, while the smile on Marcel's face immediately turns to his usual scowl when he sees me standing there.

"The galley is for crew only," I growl.

"Vas te faire enculé…" Marcel mumbles under his breath, most likely swearing, still glaring at me.

Mackenzie giggles softly, and I have the sudden urge to grab the closest plate and chuck it across the room when she rests her hand on top of Marcel's on the counter and gives it a little pat.

"She's not supposed to be down here," I mutter angrily to Marcel, but unable to take my eyes off of Mackenzie *touching him*.

I know I sound like an asshole, and I know I'm *acting* like an asshole, but I can't control it. She's too beautiful, too put-together. She's still wearing a dress from dinner that looks like it was tailor made for her body. It's form-fitting, hugs her curves, and ties up around her neck, showcasing those amazing tits I jerked-off to this afternoon. The bright white of the material brings out the tan of her skin and the blue of her eyes and makes her look clean, perfect, classy…everything that doesn't belong down in these crew quarters. She's doesn't belong in this shithole where curses are screamed, pictures of hand-drawn dicks and tits litter the walls, Marcel's sweat hangs in the air more potent than the dinner he made tonight, and where I've caught Ben getting more than one blow job over the years.

"I'm sorry, don't be mad at Marcel. I came down here on my own," Mackenzie tells me, finally moving her hand off of his and making me feel less like stabbing him in the throat with a steak knife, but still pissed off that she's even down here to begin with.

"Aren't you supposed to be over at St. John with everyone else?" I asked irritably, crossing my arms in front of me to give me something to do with my hands before I'm tempted to stalk around the counter and yank the front of her dress down so I can see just how perfect her tits really are.

"I am," she replies with a shrug. "I just couldn't handle any more family time today. I needed a break. That, and I was starving and I knew no one would let me grab anything to eat on the island since they have tons of shopping to do. Dinner was amazing, but it just wasn't my thing."

The way she sneers the word *shopping* and the annoyed look on her face gives me pause, but before I analyze the fact that she doesn't seem to share the same money spending addiction as the rest of her family, I open my mouth and more asshole comes out.

"Really? A five-course dinner that included lobster risotto and filet mignon wasn't your thing? Not fancy enough for your tastes?"

I regret the sarcastic words as soon as they leave my mouth, but it's too late to do anything about them. Marcel mutters something else in French under his breath while giving me the evil eye, and Mackenzie lifts her chin and stares at me defiantly, her eyes sparkling with anger.

"Actually, it was *too* fancy. I asked Marcel if he had anything a little simpler I could whip up myself, but he insisted on making it for me."

She points to the plate in front of her that I hadn't noticed when I walked in here, too consumed with lust and rage and all sorts of emotions I didn't know what the fuck to do with.

"A cheeseburger and french fries?" I ask in shock, staring at the half-eaten burger and only a few fries left on the plate in front of her. "You wanted a cheeseburger and fries instead of lobster and filet?"

She huffs at me in irritation and mirrors my pose, crossing her arms in front of her. Which just pushes that spectacular cleavage up even more in the sinful dress she's wearing, and my mouth waters with the need to run my tongue over the soft mounds.

"Yes, why is that so hard to believe? When I was

little, my dad and I had this thing we'd do where we always ordered a cheeseburger and fries everywhere we went and make a list of the places that had the absolute best so we knew which places we wanted to go back to," she explains, a soft wistfulness taking over her face and replacing her frustration with my attitude.

I overheard her and her dad talking about something like this last night night after dinner, but I was doing my best to pretend like Mackenzie wasn't there and didn't hear all of their conversation.

"So, who was at the top of the list?" I ask, against my better judgment.

I don't want to know these "normal" things about her. She needs to remain out of reach and out of my league, not turn into a regular, everyday cheeseburger and french fry loving woman.

She smiles at me, and God dammit, if it doesn't light up this entire fucking room and make my heart beat double time.

"Well, it used to be this little diner in Pennsylvania, but I'm pretty sure Marcel has them beat."

Marcel, the little fucker, has the nerve to blush and smile and says something to her all sweet and soft in French. She looks away from me to return his smile, and there she goes again, speaking a few little words in that foreign language that makes my dick want to jump right out of my pants and into her gorgeous mouth.

I want to tell Marcel to go the fuck away so I can

close the distance between us, lift her up and slam her ass down on the counter. I want to be alone with her so I can push between those gorgeous thighs of hers and ease some of this pain in my balls.

But I can't do that. And it just pisses me off.

"You need to go back up to the guest quarters where you belong, before you get that fancy dress stained. I'm sure it cost more than what I make in a year, and I really don't feel like giving up half my paycheck to have it cleaned for you."

Silence. Complete silence fills the room and, once again, I want to take back the shitty thing I just said, but it's too late now.

I watch as she keeps the smile on her face while she turns to Marcel and asks him if she can take the plate up to her room so she can finish her dinner there. He nods quickly, picking it up and handing it to her before she leans in and gives him a kiss on the cheek.

I keep watching, unable to move or say a word when she walks around the counter, her body brushing against mine when she moves through the small doorway to the stairs that lead back up to the guest area. The smell of coconut coming from her skin is so delicious that I have to bite down on my bottom lip to stop myself from leaning down and licking her bare shoulder, which I'm sure would earn me a smack across the face after the way I just spoke to her.

"For your information," Mackenzie suddenly says

from behind me, making me turn my head and look back over my shoulder at her while she glares at me, clutching the plate so tightly in both hands that her knuckles are white. "This dress cost $19.99 and it was from Target."

She turns and begins walking up the stairs, but not before shouting one last thing over her shoulder.

"Baise juste à côté!"

Marcel laughs loudly, and I stare at her ass as she stomps up the stairs, waiting until she disappears from sight before I turn back to him with a questioning look on my face.

For the first time in the four years I've known the man, he speaks to me in accented English.

"She just told you to fuck right off. I really, really like her."

Moving through the galley to the opposite side of the room from where Mackenzie just exited, I give Marcel the finger when I pass him and head to my bunk.

"Oh, shut the hell up."

Marcel's laughter follows me all the way down the hall.

CHAPTER 8

⚓

Mackenzie

"CAN YOU BELIEVE the nerve of him? I mean, honestly. He avoids me all day and then has a stick up his ass because I was down in his precious crew area. It's not like I care, but he didn't need to act like such an asshole," I complain to Brooke as we lay our towels down on the soft white sand of Trunk Bay Beach to relax and get some sun before it's time to head back to the boat.

We were supposed to leave this morning to cruise around the islands for a few days before we made our final stop at St. Croix, but Allyson and Arianna decided they hadn't done nearly enough shopping last night, and had my dad tell the captain to keep us at St. John for another day. I was pissed at first when I found out my dad jumped to do their bidding and didn't care that it would require more work and more planning for the captain and crew, but when I realized I wouldn't have to be stuck on the boat for another damn day where I might run into Declan, I jumped at the chance to get the hell away from him.

Sure, I stupidly stayed behind last night. And while it's true I did nothing more than push my food around my plate at dinner, and my stomach was threatening to eat itself by the time everyone left to come over here, I didn't stay behind just to have Marcel make me the most delicious cheeseburger and french fries I'd ever eaten. I stayed behind because, like an idiot, I listened to Brooke when she suggested I make up an excuse not to go with everyone so I could find Declan and make him stop avoiding me.

I never imagined that when I finally found him, or actually, when he finally found *me*, that he'd treat me the way he did and talk to me like he had. And to make matters worse, he did it in front of Marcel, who had been so sweet to make me an extra dinner and let me practice my high school French that I'd had no use for since I'd graduated.

It took everything in me not to smack Declan across the face when he made the comment about getting my dress dirty. So much for thinking it would be easy for me to show him I'm not a spoiled princess like Arianna and Allyson. It's obvious that's all he sees when he looks at me, and I wasted my time thinking I could prove him wrong. I wasted my time thinking maybe he, too, couldn't stop remembering that kiss we shared, wondering if he wanted me just as much as I wanted him. I should have stuck to my guns. I never have been, nor will I ever be, the kind of woman who can have a fling. Especially with a man who clearly hates my guts and isn't affected by me in the least.

"Yes, you've told me. At least seventy-five times since lunch," Brooke deadpans, replying to my earlier complaints as she pulls off her cover-up and flops down on her towel.

"Sorry, am I getting on your nerves? Just tell me to shut the hell up," I apologize, lying down next to her and perching myself up my elbows to look out at the crystal clear water stretched out in front of us, our yacht visible in the distance.

"Shut the hell up," Brooke mutters, covering her eyes from the sun to look up at me. "At least shut up about the whole not caring thing. You wouldn't be bitching about it all day if you didn't care. You're hot for the guy, he kissed you and made you see stars, and now you're pissed he was a jerk. I'm pissed too. I kind of want to chop off his balls when we get back on the boat, but I'll leave that up to you. It will make you feel better."

Just like always, Brooke makes me laugh and forget my problems for a minute.

"Just let me enjoy my anger for a little while longer and I promise I'll stop complaining. Right now, it feels better to be pissed off than sad," I tell her, flipping over onto my stomach to rest my chin on my arms.

"I'm sorry your dad didn't come with us today," Brooke says softly as I scoop up a handful of sand and watch it run through my fingers.

"It was stupid of me to even ask. I knew he'd pick them over me."

Not only have I felt like a fool all day for the way Declan spoke to me in front of Marcel, and how easily he dismissed me, I wanted to kick myself for letting down my guard and telling him about the road trips my dad and I used to take in search of the perfect burger and fries. Even though I regret showing him a piece of me that he didn't deserve, at least it gave me the courage to ask my dad to spend the day with me today when we were eating breakfast. I wanted him to miss spending time with me as much as I missed being with him. When I told him about how Brooke and I planned on renting bikes to ride around the small nine-mile island to see the sights, his eyes lit up and for just one minute, I thought he'd quickly agree.

But just like always, Allyson complained that she couldn't possibly shop without my father's opinion on her purchases, and Arianna wrapped her arms around his neck, called him *daddy* and told him she was looking forward to spending the whole day with him.

They didn't value his opinion, and they didn't want to spend quality time with him. The only thing they wanted was the Gold Amex in his wallet.

"Alright, no more feeling sorry for yourself. We're still on vacation and we're going to have a good time, dammit," Brooke suddenly announces.

I watch as she sits up and digs into the backpack she brought with her, pulling out two flasks. She hands me one and takes the lid off of the other before tipping it back and taking a healthy swallow. When she pulls it away from her mouth, she clunks her flask against mine and gives me a smile.

"Bottoms up, baby!" she cheers, reaching down and tipping my flask up to my mouth, forcing me to take a drink.

The rum Brooke packed burns a path down my throat, and I have to pull the flask away to cough a few times while she pats me on the back.

"That's top shelf rum Ben stole for me! They keep it locked up for guests. No one chokes on top shelf rum!" she chastises.

I shake my head at her with a smile and take another smaller sip, the burn lessening with each swallow I drink. Brooke nods her head in approval and clinks our flasks together again.

"Let's get drunk and screw. I mean, let's get drunk and come up with a way to make Declan feel like an asshole and grovel at your feet, so you can forgive him and then eventually screw him," she laughs.

I don't have the heart to tell her that's NEVER

going to happen. There is nothing he could say to me that would make me forgive him.

⚓

"ALL I CAN think about is that Goddamn kiss. Every time I close my eyes I can taste you and smell you and feel you against me, and it's driving me fucking insane."

What was I saying earlier about how there's nothing Declan could say to make me forgive him?

When Ben and Eddie picked us up from St. John and took us back to the ship, after yet another uncomfortable dinner where Allyson and Arianna occupied my dad's entire focus and talked about nothing but how much money they'd spent all day, I locked myself in mine and Brooke's room to take a shower and try to purge some of the rum from my pores. Still buzzed after my shower and finding a note on the bed from Brooke saying she went to find Ben, I threw on my pajamas of a tank top and a little pair of cotton shorts and attempted to sleep off all the rum I'd consumed.

With my head full of booze and an irritating man I couldn't get out of my thoughts no matter how hard I tried, I gave up trying to sleep and went for a walk around the ship. I should have known he'd find me just like he had the other night, but I assumed he'd be working ten times harder to avoid me after what happened in the kitchen the night before.

"Did you hear what I said?" Declan asks in a low

voice, my hands clenching tighter around the railing when I feel him move closer to me, the heat from his body practically burning a hole into my back.

"I heard you. And I don't care," I reply flippantly, finally turning around to face him and regretting it immediately.

I thought seeing Declan in his white polo shirt and khaki cargo shorts was off the charts hot, but nothing compares to him standing here in front of me in a pair of well-worn jeans that hang low on his hips and a tight, faded red t-shirt with the words "St. Thomas" written in script across his wide, sculpted chest.

He has both hands shoved into the front pockets of his jeans, pulling them down so low that I can see the white stripe of his boxer briefs that say "Calvin Klein" printed across it.

His eyes stare down at me, unblinking, and a muscle ticks in his jaw while he waits for me to say something else. Or maybe he's trying to think of a reply to me telling him I don't give a shit that he hasn't been able to stop thinking about our kiss. Whatever he's doing, I don't care. I also don't care that the muscles of his arms are flexing, and I can tell he must be clenching his hands in his pockets. Nor do I care that his spiky hair is even more messy and looks like he's been running his hands through it for hours out of irritation.

I also don't care that he's standing so close I can smell his stupid soap and his stupid spicy cologne.

When he lets out a slow, frustrated breath, I can smell his minty toothpaste, and I want to stick my tongue in his mouth and lick it off his teeth.

Jesus God, what is wrong with me?

"Turn around," he suddenly orders.

I look away from his throat, getting momentarily distracted by the bobbing of his Adam's apple when he swallowed, and stare up at him in confusion.

"Excuse me?"

He closes the few inches of distance between us until he's in my space, crowding me and making it hard for me to breathe. He slowly pulls his hands out of his pockets and I hold my breath, wondering if he's going to put them on me.

Instead, he leans towards me and rests his hands on either side of me on the railing, caging me in.

"I said, turn around. I can't say what I need to say when you're looking at me like that," he tells me, his voice going lower, deeper, and flipping a switch between my legs that feels like a bolt of electricity just hit me.

"Looking at you like what?" I whisper, forcing myself not to grab onto handfuls of his shirt and drag his mouth down to mine.

"Like you can't keep your hands off me," he replies, the corner of his mouth tipping up in a smirk, exchanging my lust for the need to bring my knee up between his legs, even if what he said IS true.

"You've got a lot of nerve. I can't believe you—"

"Mackenzie! Just turn the fuck around...please." He cuts me off.

I would have ignored him and continued telling him where he could shove his orders, but there was something about the way he said please, so guttural and needy, that my body reacted without thinking.

Wetting my lips with my tongue to get rid of the dryness that occurred, not only from hearing the way he said please, but also hearing him say my name as well, he lets out a low groan as his eyes track the movement of my tongue before I slowly turn away from him.

I see his hands tighten on the railing on either side of me as I take my time, my shoulder sliding against his chest and my hip grazing across the hardness in his jeans as I turn back around to face the dark ocean stretched out beyond us. It makes me feel good that I have this effect on him when I thought he was immune to me, but that doesn't mean I'm going to stand here all night taking his orders. He's got five seconds to explain himself or I'm ducking out from under his arms and going back to my room.

Once again, he closes what little distance there was between us until his chest is flush with my back and I can feel his cock through his jeans, nestled right against my ass. He bends his head down to the side of my face, nuzzling his nose against my cheek and using it to push my hair away until his lips are right by my ear.

"All I can think about is that Goddamn kiss. Every

time I close my eyes I can taste you, and smell you, and feel you against me, and it's driving me fucking insane."

He repeats the same words he said to me when he first came out here and found me standing in the same position just moments ago, but this time he whispers them and his warm breath skates over my ear, making me break out in goosebumps.

"W-what's your point?" I stutter, trying to make my voice sound strong and clear, like the way his lips are just barely touching my earlobe isn't driving me completely insane.

"My point, Mackenzie, is that I can't kiss you again. I can't touch you again. I can't taste you again. You're a guest; I'm on the crew. I can't cross that line with you and it's fucking killing me," he whispers into my ear, his hips jerking forward and his cock digging deeper into my ass, letting me know just how much it's really killing him.

It's not the apology I had been hoping for, but the need in his voice and the whites of his knuckles holding onto the railing, keeping me caged in, prove that it's taking all of his strength not to kiss me, not to touch me, and not to taste me. Maybe I'm a pathetic, weak woman, but I don't need an apology anymore. He just admitted why he acted the way he did without coming right out and saying the words. Obviously there are rules about guests and crew members hooking up, and he's having a really hard time wanting to break those rules. He acted like an asshole last night because it probably pissed him off that I made him want to cross the line and he didn't know how to handle it.

I can work with that. I can forgive his asshole behavior for something like that, but it doesn't mean I'm going to let him off easy. He's still rubbing his cock against me and breathing in my ear. I'm surrounded by him and his smell, and I'm so wet right now I'd probably come faster than I ever have in my life if he broke his stupid rules and touched me.

"So, let's pretend," I whisper, craning my neck around until he has to pull his mouth away from my ear so he can look down at my face.

I push myself up on my toes until my mouth is right by his and our lips are just barely touching, his eyes darkening as they stare down at me.

"Let's pretend I'm not a guest, and you're not on the crew. We're just two people who happen to be on the same boat," I speak softly against his mouth. "What would you do to me then?"

He doesn't answer me right away, and nothing but the sound of the ship racing through the water can be heard over the thumping of my heart. The muscles in my legs start to shake as I continue holding myself up so I can be close to his mouth, and right when I think he's going to push away from me and storm off like he did the other night after he kissed me, he gives me that damn smirk again.

"Put your hands on the railing. And hold on tight," he finally whispers back.

CHAPTER 9

Declan

I'M THE BIGGEST hypocrite in the world. I bitch at Ben all the time about mixing business with pleasure, and what the fuck do I do within ten seconds of being close to Mackenzie? I've got her pinned against the railing and my cock pressed against her ass, whispering in her ear and trying not to blow my load with how damn good she smells. I swear to Christ she must bathe in suntan lotion.

At least my intentions were good when I initially came out here, intent on finding her so I could try to explain why I acted the way I did the night before. I rehearsed what I would say a thousand times in my head after I heard the jetty come back a few hours ago. I paced the entire length of the ship ten times after all my nightly duties were finished and I was officially off the clock until morning, hoping Mackenzie would believe it when I told her that I just wasn't interested, the kiss meant nothing, and I couldn't be distracted by anyone or anything while I was working.

And then I came around the corner and found her leaning against the railing, just like the night I kissed her, her hair still damp from a shower as the ocean breeze got a hold of it and blew it around her face. I couldn't take my eyes off her long, smooth legs or her perfect ass in those tiny cotton shorts. I moved up behind her, got a whiff of her coconut skin, and everything I planned to say flew from my mind.

I admitted I couldn't stop thinking about that damn kiss. I told her every time I closed my eyes I could taste her, smell her, and feel her, like the Goddamn pussy I am. I thought when I explained how she's a guest, I'm on the crew, and we couldn't cross that line, that would be it. She'd understand and walk away, not torment me by rubbing her body against mine or whispering against my lips, wanting me to pretend like we were other people.

I'm the biggest hypocrite in the world, and right now, I don't give a fuck.

"Put your hands on the railing. And hold on tight," I whisper, watching Mackenzie give me a smirk of her own before turning her head away from me and doing what I ask.

Her wet hair continues to blow around between us, and I take one hand off the railing to gather it up in in my fist, holding it down by the nape of her neck before bending my head and putting my mouth back by her ear.

"If you weren't a guest, and I wasn't on the crew, I'd slide my hand around your waist and touch those couple of inches of bare skin showing below the edge of your tank top that have been driving me crazy since I saw you standing here," I speak against her ear.

I watch her hands tighten on the railing in front of her as I do just what I said. My palm slides against the warm skin of her lower stomach where her tank top had risen up, stopping just over her belly button to add some pressure and pull her ass back harder against my cock.

"What else?" she whispers, her voice floating away with the breeze as I smile at the rapid rise and fall of her chest, her breath coming out faster the more I talk.

"I'd finally taste your skin, and see if you tasted as sweet as I imagined," I reply, dipping my head down lower.

I scrape my teeth against the side of her neck before easing the sting with my lips, gently sucking her skin into my mouth and swirling my tongue around the area I just bit.

Mackenzie whimpers softly, and her hips start to move as she rubs her ass slowly against my cock before demanding more.

"What else?"

I continue sucking on her neck for a few seconds before I make a trail of kisses back up to her ear and reply.

"If we were other people, I'd slide my hand up under your shirt and finally touch those amazing tits I jerked off to when I saw you rubbing lotion on them yesterday."

She makes a noise somewhere between a shocked gasp and a strangled moan as my hand slowly makes its way up under her tank top, gliding against the soft skin of her stomach and wanting to scream to the heavens in thanks that she's not wearing a bra.

It's my turn to let out a guttural moan when my hand palms one of her bare breasts, kneading the heavy weight of it in my hand before grazing my thumb back and forth across the tight bud of her nipple.

"Did you really jerk off after you saw me, or are we still pretending?" Mackenzie asks, letting out another small sound of pleasure when I pinch her nipple gently between my thumb and forefinger.

Hearing her say the words "jerk off" makes me want to shove my hand down my pants and do exactly that, but this is all about her right now. She's letting me do these things to her after I was a Grade A asshole. I'm not about to fuck it up by pleasuring myself instead of her.

"I locked myself down in my bunk and came so hard I almost saw stars," I admit, tugging and pulling on her nipple before moving my hand away and back down the skin of her stomach.

I keep my hand still, running my fingertips back and forth over her skin, right above the waistband of her shorts, waiting for her to say the words. It only takes her a few seconds to realize I'm not going to do anything else until she does.

"What else?" she finally asks.

I know I should draw this out, make it longer and make it worth it for her. I've already decided this is it with Mackenzie. Just this one time, just this one taste and then we can both stop pretending. I can get my fucking head back on straight and do my job without the distraction of wondering what she sounds like and feels like when she comes, and she can go back to enjoying the rest of her vacation without worrying about me pissing her off.

I know I should take my time, but I can't. It's impossible. I want it all and I want it now.

"I'd try my hardest to take it slow, but I wouldn't be able to stop myself from pushing my hands down into those tight little shorts and finding out if you're wet for me."

My hand immediately moves, acting out my words as my fingers dip beneath the waistband of her shorts and her lacy underwear, not stopping until they come in contact with her smoothly waxed, hot pussy, and I find out the answer to what I was wondering.

She's so wet, my fingers easily glide through her folds and we both moan at the same time when I stop, holding the tips right at her pulsing center.

"W-what else?" she stutters as one of her hands comes off the railing to clutch tightly to my arm that's wrapped around her waist and down inside her shorts.

"I'd fuck you with my fingers until you came and I could hear you shout my name," I tell her as her fingernails dig into the skin of my forearm, trying to push me to act on the words I just spoke.

A strangled sound of need comes out of her mouth when I hold my hand still, refusing to move until she tells me something first.

"What are you doing? Keep going," she begs softly, her face turning towards mine as my fingers lazily swirl against her wet heat, building up her need, wanting her crazy with it so she'll know exactly how I've felt since the first moment I saw her.

"Tell me what Marcel called me under his breath when I found you guys in the galley."

Her eyes widen in shock as she pulls her head back to look up at me.

"Seriously? You want to talk about Marcel right now?"

I start to pull my fingers away from her, and she digs her nails into me so hard I'm pretty sure she might have drawn blood.

"Fine! He said *Fuck you, motherfucker*," she shouts in

irritation, the swear words coming out of her perfect little mouth making me laugh and turning me on even more than I thought possible. "Are you finished? Can we get back to—"

I lean down and press my lips to hers, quickly thrusting two fingers inside of her at the same time. She lets out a shocked moan into my mouth and I hold myself still inside of her to give her a second to get used to me invading her body, and to give myself some time to calm the fuck down before I thrust my cock against her ass and come in my jeans.

She's so wet and tight and perfect. I push my tongue past her lips and pull my fingers almost all the way out of her before quickly thrusting them back in as deep as I can go. Her tongue tangles with mine and I swallow her whimpers of need as I fuck her pussy with my fingers, adding my thumb to circle around her swollen clit.

Her hips thrust up against my hand, begging me to fuck her faster and deeper. I clench her hair more tightly in my fist to bring her head back farther so I can kiss her harder, my fingers never stopping the rough push and pull out of her body. She presses her hand harder against my arm, helping me move faster between her thighs until I can hear the wet slapping of my fingers as I take everything she's willing to give me.

I push away the depressing thought that this will be the one and only time I can let this happen and concentrate on sliding my tongue through her mouth and pleasuring her with my hand, the only thing I can give her right now.

Moving my mouth away from hers, I kiss my way to her ear.

"Say something in French," I whisper, keeping my fingers buried inside of her to lazily swirl my thumb around her clit, loving the way her hips jerk against my hand, begging me to keep moving.

"Tu le sens si bien. N'arrête pas. You feel so good. Don't stop," she speaks quickly in a soft voice, translating the words for me and ending with a low moan when I press my thumb harder against her clit as I rub little circles around it.

"Christ, that's so fucking hot," I mutter against her ear, moving my fingers between her legs faster, knowing if she doesn't come soon, I'm going to rip these fucking shorts off her legs and slam my cock inside of her.

I've never felt so tied up in knots over *anyone* before. I've never wanted to risk *everything* just for one taste and one touch of a woman before. I can't even bother feeling a second of regret. I stop worrying about what will happen when I tell her this was a one-time thing, when I feel Mackenzie's pussy start to tighten around my fingers and she gets impossibly wetter.

I move my mouth away from hers and thrust my fingers deeply, holding them perfectly still as I curl those two fingers up inside of her. The tips of my fingers press against her g-spot as my thumb continues to work her clit, swiping back and forth over it until she squeezes her eyes closed and her head falls back against my shoulder.

"Let me hear it. Let me hear you say my name when you come," I tell her, my thumb moving faster and my hand letting go of the hold it has on her hair to wrap around her waist and anchor her body to me.

Her hips jerk erratically against my hand and I start thrusting my fingers in and out of her again until it happens. Her tight pussy pulses around my fingers and she opens her mouth, shouting my name into the night sky.

"Oh, my God, Declan...I'm coming. Fuck, Declan!"

I soak up the sound of my name on her lips, knowing I'll never, ever forget it. I hold my arm around her body tighter and my fingers continue pumping in and out of her, drawing out her orgasm until her hips finally stop jerking and her body falls forward, both of her arms smacking down on the railing to cushion the slump of her head onto them.

Even though I never want to leave the heat of her body, I slowly draw my fingers out of her, pulling her tank top back down and straightening the waistband of her shorts, chuckling to myself when I hear her let out a long, exhausted moan.

"Holy shit," she mutters, her voice muffled against

her arms while she's still bent forward in front of me. "If that was pretend, what the hell would you do to me if it were real?"

CHAPTER 10

$\large\unicode{x2693}$

Mackenzie

WE'VE BEEN CRUISING around the islands for a day and a half, taking our time to get to St. Croix. I tried not to let it bother me that, once again, Declan has performed a fabulous disappearing act and I've only seen him from a distance a small handful of times. Each time I headed in his direction or tried to catch his eye, he'd move to another part of the boat or disappear inside somewhere.

This guy is getting on my last nerve, and he's making me feel like an idiot for letting down my guard with him AGAIN. The only reason I haven't hunted him down and made him say something to me is because I can't fully hate the guy for giving me the best damn orgasm I've had in my life, followed by the best sleep I've had in months.

Not even the twin terrors could kill my buzz yesterday morning over breakfast when they told me the sundress I was wearing was tacky and made me look washed out. I didn't even bat an eye at them after lunch when they told me I was started to look a little "thick in the thighs" and shouldn't be eating so much on vacation. They were just pissed because Marcel gave them the boring Kale salad with tasteless fat free dressing on the side they requested, and he made me, my father, and Brooke an entire tray of sliders and a giant basket of french fries. While the three of us inhaled the greasy, fried and delicious food, laughing and having a good time, Allyson and Brooke stabbed their forks at their stupid salads and glared at us the entire time.

I pretended like I wasn't looking for Declan all day yesterday, like I wasn't trying to figure out a way to ask him if we could have a repeat performance as soon as possible. I let Brooke distract me by having Ben set up the water trampoline for us when the captain anchored the boat for a little while and made sure we used it for an obscene amount of time to make it worth his effort. I pretended like I wasn't jealous in the least that Ben did everything in his power to be near Brooke, switching jobs with anyone he could so he could hang out with us. He was nice and funny, and I liked that he made my best friend smile and laugh and had no problem putting up with her sarcasm. Even if Brooke would never see or speak to him again when this trip was over, it was nice to see her happy and relaxed and not always worrying about me. I also did a good job pretending like I didn't wish Ben's easy-going attitude and how he said exactly what he was thinking would rub off on Declan.

My good mood lasted until last night at dinner when I waited for Declan to show up. He had to bartend again, which meant he couldn't avoid me. A few minutes before our first course arrived, Ben came rushing out onto the deck, apologizing for being late, explaining that Declan had other things to do tonight and he'd be taking over as bartender. For a second, I thought maybe this was Ben's way to hang around Brooke again, but when he looked over at me and gave me a sheepish smile and an apologetic shrug, I knew Declan must have said something to him and this had everything to do with me.

I went to bed early in a bad mood, tossing and turning until the sun came up this morning.

To add to my exhaustion and overall irritability today, I got a phone call from one of my father's attorney's telling me it was imperative that I check my email as soon as possible and reply back to him immediately. I've been walking all over this damn ship trying to get a Wi-Fi signal and nothing is working.

With my head down as I hold my laptop in one hand and bang on the keys with another, I make my way off the sundeck and inside to the main salon. Setting my computer down on the bar top in the corner, I check the Wi-Fi signal again and curse under my breath when it's still not available.

"Having troubles?"

Even though I'm pissed at him right now, the sound of Declan's low, gravelly voice behind me still makes my skin tingle and reminds me of all the wonderful and dirty things he said in my ear the other night.

"Yes. The stupid Wi-Fi on this boat isn't working and I have something important I need to check," I reply, not bothering to turn around as I continue to smack they keys in annoyance.

"Something important to check on vacation? What, like a really *fabulous* shoe sale?"

The sarcasm and outright loathing in his voice shocks me completely speechless. Gone is the man who whispered hot words of need and want in my ear, who touched me like he'd been doing it for years and knew exactly what to do to bring me the most pleasure. The back of my eyes prickle with tears and I curse myself a thousand different ways for letting some guy I just met get under my skin like this.

"Don't worry, princess, the shoes will still be there in a few days. I'm sure you'll manage."

The meanness in his voice that I've done nothing to deserve, quickly dries up my unshed tears and makes me stand up a little taller as I slowly turn around and face him.

I hate that he looks so good in his navy blue polo

TARA SIVEC

and shorts. I hate that I know exactly what his mouth tastes like, the one that just spoke to me in such a shitty way. I hate that I'm letting a stupid vacation fling, which hasn't even really turned into a fling, drive me so crazy that I want to scream. I hate that he's standing here in front of me, staring at me with a condescending smirk on his face when I can't stop thinking about how good he looks. I'll be damned if I sit here and take it.

"Sure. Because that's all I do. Sit around and spend money, right?" I ask in a chipper, sarcastic voice, watching the smirk quickly die on his face. "I couldn't possibly have a brain in my head or actual important things to handle that could affect my family's entire life, could I? I just sit on my ass, ordering people around, and spending my father's money just like the two raging bitches outside, right? That's what you see when you look at me, right? RIGHT?"

I'm shouting now and I know it's only a matter of time before someone hears us and comes running in here, but I don't give a shit. I'm tired of people looking at me seeing what they want to see instead of what's really there. I'm tired of letting people walk over me and never having a voice. Fuck them and fuck *him*.

"Damn, you got me there. It's amazing how well you know me after only FIVE FUCKING DAYS!" I finish.

Declan winces and at least has the nerve to look properly chastised and a little bit ashamed. Or maybe he's just shocked by my outburst. Either way, when he opens his mouth, I quickly cut him off, holding up my hand to silence him before I turn around and slam the lid to my laptop closed. I scoop it up in my arms and turn back to face him, stalking across the room and right past him, his mouth still opening and closing like he's trying to come up with something to say.

"Save it," I mutter when I hear him whisper my name. "One orgasm isn't worth having to listen to whatever bullshit is about to come out of your mouth."

He doesn't try to say anything after that and lets me walk out of the main salon with my head held high, even though I want to curl up in a ball and cry.

By the time I make it to my room and slam the door closed behind me, I flop down on my bed and open up my laptop to see I finally have a signal. I quickly open up my email and scroll through all the ones I've missed in the last few days until I get to the most recent one.

Opening it up, I quickly scan through the document and my heart drops to my toes. I wanted to be right so badly. I wanted to have proof in my hands that I could take to my father, and here it is, in black and white. I have the proof I needed, but nothing about this makes me feel good. Knowing what I have to do and what I have to say to my father makes a knot form in my stomach I feel will never go away. The pain in my stomach grows tenfold when I can't stop picturing the look on Declan's face a little bit ago or the way he spoke to me.

Shoving the laptop across the bed, I scoot up to the pillows, lie down on my side and hug my knees to my chest, wanting nothing more than to forget about what I just saw. It's all too much right now and I can't take it anymore. Six months has led up to this moment right here. Six months of barely eating, barely sleeping, working all hours of the night, and not having a life have finally come to a head. I'm about to ruin my father's life, and yet I can't stop thinking about Declan McGillis, and why it hurts so much that he can't see past my family's money to the person I really am.

It's bad enough I've let my stepmother and stepsister treat me like shit, and I've let my father ignore me and his mounting problems. It's down right pathetic I let a guy I've only known for a few days make me feel worse.

CHAPTER 11

Declan

I HEAR A low whistle from behind me and look away from the door Mackenzie just exited to find Brooke standing in the open, sliding doorway that leads out to the sundeck. As if it wasn't bad enough I made the mistake of crossing the line with a guest, something I've never done in my career, I also had a witness to my asshole behavior when I tried to fix things in the most fucked up way imaginable.

I got caught up in the moment with Mackenzie, thinking I could take what I'd been craving since I first laid eyes on her and then move on and do my job, but that was impossible. I couldn't stop thinking about her; I couldn't stop wanting her and wanting *more* and it fucked with my head. I woke up yesterday morning with my thoughts a jumbled mess, wondering what she was thinking, what she was doing, where she was on the ship, and if she was replaying everything that had happened the night before and hungering for more just like I was. For the first time in four years, I got my ass chewed out by the captain. I screwed up the hand signals helping him lift anchor, I forgot to clean the windows for him in the wheelhouse, and neglected a whole other laundry list of duties I've always stayed on top of. All because I couldn't stop thinking about the sound of Mackenzie saying my name when she came.

"You're a dick," she says, stating the obvious.

"I'm sorry. That was completely unprofessional of me."

Brooke laughs softly, but there's no trace of humor on her face as she shakes her head at me.

"I'm not the one you should be apologizing to, and I don't give a rat's ass about you being unprofessional. I'm not gonna go tattling on you to the captain."

I let out a small sigh of relief, even though I know that's not what I should be the most concerned with right now. Instead of talking to Mackenzie like a man, I took the pussy way out by treating her like shit to push her away. Avoiding her after the captain verbally kicked my ass worked for a little while. I was able to get back to work and stop hearing the echoes of her moans in my head or still feel how tightly her body gripped around my fingers, but as soon as I walked into this room and saw her standing by the bar, muttering angry curses under her breath at her computer, it all came crashing back and I forgot how to breathe. She wore a sheer cover-up over that fucking blue bikini, but I could still clearly see every inch of her gorgeous body underneath. The same body I'd touched and been inside of. Her thick, dark hair was up in a messy bun on top of her head with pieces falling down around her face, but I could still see the smooth expanse of her neck. The same one I'd nipped with my teeth and tasted with my tongue.

When my dick instantly hardened for her, it pissed me off that I had no control whenever I was within ten feet of that woman. She made me forget about my job, she made me disregard my dreams and almost throw away everything I'd worked so hard for. She made me want to break all of my own rules and not give a shit about the consequences. I had every intention of telling her what happened was a one-time thing, apologize for acting unprofessionally and assure her I wouldn't do anything else to screw up the rest of her vacation, but it all flew out the fucking window when my dick had other ideas and I lashed out at her.

"Let's just get something straight here, buddy," Brooke continues. "I know you look at my friend and you see a woman who's led a privileged life and that seems to piss you off for some reason, but you don't know one Goddamn thing about her."

What she's saying to me isn't really a surprise. Even though the rest of her family acts like entitled assholes, I knew within the first couple of minutes of meeting her she was different from them. But that doesn't mean she hasn't had an easy life. It doesn't mean she hasn't had things handed to her on a silver platter that other people had to bust their ass for. Sure, she's not a bitch and she appreciates people who do things for her and actually has manners, but we live in completely different worlds. She doesn't know the first thing about sacrifice or worrying about screwing up a job that you depend on to pay the bills and to make your dreams come true. All of these differences between us become more glaringly obvious with each day that passes. I know I handled it all wrong, but the facts are still there. I refuse to ignore them just because she's the hottest woman I've ever met.

"I know enough," I reply in irritation, not wanting to get into this with Mackenzie's best friend.

"No, you don't. You see what you want to see. I know you guys just met, and I know whatever this thing is between you two isn't going to turn into some happily ever after bullshit, but that still doesn't give you the right to judge her," Brooke fires back. "I thought it would be good for her to have a little fling with a hot guy on vacation. Something easy and fun that would take her mind off of things, but you want to make it more complicated and difficult, and she doesn't need that shit right now, especially from you."

I scoff, and now it's my turn to shake my head at

her.

"Especially from me? A poor, lowly deckhand who wasn't born with a silver spoon in his mouth?" I argue, my anger rising even though I know I'm doing it again. Forgetting about my professionalism and letting my emotions take over.

"Oh, please, that whole 'Woe is me' act doesn't work, and frankly, it just makes you look pathetic. You're talking to a woman who was born to middle class parents. My father worked in an automotive factory all his life and my mother was a kindergarten teacher," Brooke explains. "And you'd know Mackenzie wasn't born with a fucking silver spoon in her mouth if you actually took a few minutes to get to know her instead of making snap judgments just because of who her family is."

Brooke takes a minute to close the sliding glass door behind her and moves further into the room until she's standing right in front of me. I should just send her back outside and try to hold onto whatever miniscule amount of professional behavior I have left, but part of me wants to hear what she has to say. Part of me wants to see how she could possibly prove me wrong.

"Did you know her father didn't hit it big until she was a senior in high school? Up until that point, they lived in the same two-bedroom cottage he bought with her mother when they got married. Up until he sold his first app, they lived paycheck-to-paycheck, barely scraping by. Did you also know that she paid her own way through college working two jobs and taking out a shit-ton of student loans?" Brooke asks. "Because even though her father finally had money, she refused to take a hand-out from him, and he refused to have a spoiled brat for a daughter who didn't know how to work for what she wanted."

My indignation slowly starts to wilt with every word Brooke says, making feel like an even bigger asshole when she doesn't stop, digging the knife even deeper into my chest.

"Sure, when she graduated college she was hired at her father's company, but she went through the same interview process as everyone else and makes the same amount of money everyone in her department makes," Brooke informs me. "She's still trying to pay off her student loans, she gives all her free time to charity, and she works her ass off for every shitty penny she earns, in a job that makes her miserable and one she only took because she knew it would make her father happy to have her close. And I'm not even going to get into the shit she's been going through with her father the last six months and the toll it's taken on her and the stress that has kept her up nights, and how she's forgotten how to have a life. That's not my story to tell, but maybe if you hadn't been a gigantic ASSHOLE, she would have shared it with you."

I can't do anything but stand here and take it. I feel

like the shittiest person on the planet, and I deserve Brooke's anger.

"Mackenzie doesn't care if you're a *'poor deckhand'* or the richest man in the world. She cares about what type of person you are. She cares whether or not you're a decent human being. Being hot as balls is also a bonus," Brooke adds, finally giving me a small smile to alleviate the tension in the room. "She was attracted to you. She wanted to have some fun and let you help her forget about her troubles while she was stuck on this ship with Bitch One and Bitch Two and a father who has forgotten she exists. Period. You don't want people to judge you because you don't have a shit-ton of money to throw around? Then stop judging people who *do*."

With that, she turns and heads back to the sliding door, making me feel even worse than I did when I first opened my mouth and spewed my judgment all over a woman who definitely didn't deserve it.

Brooke pauses with her hand on the glass door, looking back over her shoulder at me.

"When you finally decide to pull your head out of your ass, try using the words 'I'm sorry, I was wrong.' Maybe even practice it in the mirror a few times and try not to look constipated when you say them," she informs me. "Mackenzie is a pretty forgiving person, and I still think you could be good for her once you get that stick out of your ass and actually get to know her. Don't fuck it up this time or I'll chop off your balls and make you eat them."

Brooke gives me a small wave over her shoulder as she leaves, and even though her words make me want to cover my balls and guard them with my life, at least she managed to make me smile.

Formulating a plan that hopefully won't get me fired, I race out of the main salon in search of Ben and Eddie, hoping they'll cover for me for a little while so I can make everything right.

CHAPTER 12

⚓

Mackenzie

"EXCUSE ME, MISS Talbot? Could I possibly steal Miss Armstrong from you for a little while?"

I refuse to turn around when I hear Declan's voice behind me, cursing my body for betraying me when it makes a tingle go up my spine. Sitting Indian-style facing Brooke on the huge couch at the front of the ship down below the captain's wheelhouse, I clutch the playing cards tighter in my hand, concentrating on the game of blackjack we'd started an hour ago instead of the idiot man with the hot voice.

"I don't know, I'm about to kick her ass with this hand," Brooke tells him.

I shoot her a dirty look behind my sunglasses for acknowledging his presence after I told her what he said to me, and for assuming she could ever kick my ass in blackjack.

"I promise I'll bring her back and you can kick her ass then," Declan replies, and I can practically hear the smile in his voice.

First, he's a judgmental asshole, and now he's a traitor. If I hadn't already decided I was finished wasting my time with him after the pity party I gave myself in my room earlier, this would have put the final nail in his coffin.

"Ahhhhh, grasshopper CAN be taught," Brooke mutters.

I silently watch her give the man behind me a smile and a wink and I want to ask her what the hell is going on, but again—done wasting my time, don't give a shit, and all that nonsense.

"I'm a little busy here. And I need to talk to my dad," I remind Brooke, even though I've put off talking to him all afternoon.

The idea that I'd much rather ruin my father's life than spend even one second with Declan McGillis should have me questioning my sanity, but I'm already well aware of how stupid and insane I've let this man I just met make me.

"Your dad went to go lie down and take a nap while the blonde bimbos are face down on the couches in the main salon, sleeping off their day-drinking hangovers. You've got nothing but time," Brooke reminds me, grabbing the cards out of my hands and collecting the rest that are strewn all over the cushions between us.

When I finally emerged from my room, going over how I would explain everything to my dad to make it as easy as possible on him, worrying how no matter what I said, he wouldn't take it very well, I found Brooke apologizing to Zoe and telling her the two women were officially cut off from any more alcohol the rest of the day. I have no idea what happened while I was gone, and I didn't want to know. The pissed-off look on Zoe's face, the annoyance on Brooke's while we watched Jessica scoop up broken glass from the deck, and Allyson and Arianna standing off to the side pointing and laughing at her gave me enough to fill in the blanks about what I'd missed.

I was more than a little shocked when my father actually stepped forward and told them both in a stern voice, I've never heard him use with them before, that it was time for them to go inside and sleep off the alcohol. When he continued to stand there glaring at them angrily, they smartly decided to keep their mouths shut and do what he said. I didn't even realize I'd been standing there quietly with my mouth wide open until the three of them disappeared inside and Brooke made a comment about hell freezing over and my dad finally finding his balls again.

Instead of immediately going in search for him to get what I needed to say over with, Brooke suggested a game of cards so I could give him some time to cool off after having to deal with the two embarrassing women and give myself time to get my thoughts in order.

Declan suddenly enters my line of vision, moving to stand next to me on the couch and holdng his hand out for me to take.

"Please? I promise I'll only keep you off the boat for a little bit, and we'll be back before they wake up," Declan says softly.

"Are you planning on jumping over the railing while we're moving? I could give you a push if you'd like," I reply sarcastically, unable to stop myself from answering him, even though I vowed to ignore him for the rest of the trip.

I make the mistake of finally tipping my head up to look at him, and I grit my teeth when he smiles down at me. It's bad enough I want to punch his dimples right off his cheeks, now he has to torture me by wearing a tight, light blue, long-sleeved swim shirt that hugs every damn muscle in his chest and arms. His matching blue and white, Hawaiian-print board-shorts-style swim trunks hang low on his hips and I really hate the guy for giving me all these conflicting feelings of hatred and lust.

"Um, considering we stopped about thirty minutes ago and dropped anchor, I don't think I'd suffer serious harm if I jumped overboard. Even if you pushed me."

Glancing away from his stupid smiling face long enough to look beyond him, I realize he's telling the truth when I don't see the blur of the ocean as we move through it. Everything is still and calm and I feel like an idiot that I was so distracted by thoughts of my dad and Declan that I didn't even notice we'd come to a stop.

"Captain saw some bad weather up ahead and decided to wait it out in calmer waters and hope it'll move around us by sundown," Declan explains, still holding his hand out for me to take.

I don't want to go anywhere with him. I can see it written all over his face that he wants to apologize for what he said to me earlier, but I don't give a shit what he has to say. He means nothing to me. He was going to be a quick vacation fling and that's it. If he wants to think I'm a spoiled princess and treat me like dirt because of it, I don't care. Crossing my arms in front of me, I refuse to accept the hand he continues to offer and the olive branch he's trying to extend.

"You'll have to excuse my friend, she's a little stubborn. I think we might need a little more to sweeten the pot before she gives in," Brooke tells him with another damn wink that makes me want to shove *her* overboard.

"I thought we could go out on one of the jet skis and check out the coral reef a few miles from here," he replies.

"A ride on a jet ski is not going to erase your asshole behavior that I did nothing to warrant," I fire back through clenched teeth, my irritation and words making it glaringly obvious that I *do* care what he thinks of me and my feelings were hurt, even if I want to deny it.

"I'll let you drive."

Goddammit.

Of course, he has to entice me with one of the things I requested for this trip when we were filling out the questionnaire about our likes and dislikes so the crew could make sure we enjoyed our time on the ship. Sure, it wasn't much, and it was nothing nearly as extravagant as some of the things Allyson and Arianna requested, like a stupid twelve-course meal that didn't include any food that was red or green, and a masseuse to be brought out to us in the middle of the ocean every damn day so they didn't miss their hot stone massages or fall behind in their waxing, but aside from swimming with dolphins, it was the only other thing I could think of that I'd never done and wanted to try.

Knowing Declan would probably stand here all day until I give up, and really, really wanting to drive my own jet ski, I let out a huge, annoyed sigh, unable to believe that I'm actually giving in to this asshole.

Unfolding my legs and pushing myself up from the couch, I smack his offered hand away, just to make myself feel better and let him know in no uncertain terms I'm not happy about this situation. I'm only going along with it so he can say whatever he has to say to ease his conscience, and I can go back to pretending like he doesn't exist and doesn't matter.

"Let's get this over with," I mutter, brushing past him. "But if I go too fast and you fall off the back, I'm leaving you there and letting you drown."

CHAPTER 13

⚓

Declan

EVEN THOUGH MACKENZIE clearly wanted to punch my face, and I could tell she'd rather do anything else instead of go somewhere alone with me, I thanked God that my jet ski idea actually worked.

When I sucked up my pride and went in search of Ben to apologize for always getting on his case about rules, and to admit just how royally I'd fucked up and to ask him for advice. I found Zoe helping him pull out extra cases of liquor from the storage area at the back of the ship to restock the crew pantry, since Mackenzie's relatives had depleted our stock today.

When I finished explaining everything to the both of them, Ben just laughed at me and Zoe punched me in the arm. Not only did she think I'd behaved like a complete asshole, she'd had to deal with Ashley pestering her twenty-four-seven, asking her if she knew why I'd been avoiding her and if it had anything to do with the way she caught me staring at Mackenzie a few times. So much for thinking I was doing a good job hiding how much I wanted her.

I told Ben to shut the hell up and I apologized to Zoe, promising her I'd have a talk with Ashley and get her off Zoe's case as soon as I could. One problem at a time. Right now, my problem with Mackenzie was my main concern.

As soon as Ben brought up the idea of taking her somewhere on a jet ski since the ship would be stopped for the rest of the day, I forgave him for laughing at my predicament. Zoe agreed with the idea, even though she still thought I was an idiot for deciding I couldn't pursue anything else with Mackenzie for obvious reasons.

She got that even though I *wanted* to take that risk, there was too much at stake for me to do it. My main goal in getting Mackenzie alone needed to be for me to apologize for my behavior and make sure she knew, in a nicer way than what I'd already attempted and failed, that it couldn't happen again. And really, with the dirty looks she gave me and the way she smacked my hand away when I tried to help her up from the couch, I'm pretty sure even if I decided to say "fuck it" and let whatever happens, happen, Mackenzie wanted none of that anymore.

It took every ounce of willpower I had not to drop

to my knees and change my mind when we got to the railing where I'd had Ben toss over the ladder that would take us down to water level and the waiting jet ski he'd left tied up to the side of the boat.

After I threw on a life jacket and stood there holding Mackenzie's in my hand, I had to count to ten in my head and mentally tell my dick to calm the fuck down when she pulled the cover-up off her body and tossed it to her feet. She stood in front of me defiantly with her hands on her hips, wearing nothing but that blue string bikini and I had to keep my shaking hands steady when I helped her into her life jacket instead of running them all over her body like I wanted to.

When I went over the side of the railing and down the ladder first, I had to concentrate on every step I took to avoid falling into the water while I stared up at her barely-covered ass and those gorgeous long legs as she followed me down.

Let's not even talk about how difficult it was to put my hands on her hips and give her a boost up onto the jet ski once we got down in the water, or how good it felt to get on the seat behind her and feel her body nestled between my thighs. I tried as hard as I could to hide the shakiness in my voice while I leaned forward and scooted closer to her to start up the engine and give her a quick rundown on how the jet ski worked.

Hoping she couldn't feel my permanent hard-on nestled against her ass, I clutched tightly to the safety bar behind me with one hand. Even though I could have put them both there to hold on, I tortured myself by wrapping my other arm around her waist and holding her securely against me. It was part need to touch her no matter what my convictions were, and part fear for my life since true to her word, as soon as Mackenzie revved the engine and took off, she tried her hardest to chuck me off the back of the damn thing.

As pissed as she was at me, she couldn't hide her excitement or how much fun the thrill of racing through the crystal clear water was. Her squeals of delight echoed over the sound of the engine, and her laughter shook her entire body as she flew us up and over the waves from the wake she cut through the water.

When we got close to the coral reef, I removed my arm from around her waist long enough to point it out to her and told her to slow down before the water got too shallow and we plowed into the sand. She took her hand off the gas and we floated to a stop a few feet from the reef. Keeping one foot on the ledge of the ski and swinging my leg around and off the seat, I held the jet ski stable with one hand as I hopped off and held my other hand out to help her down.

All of her happiness from just a few seconds ago disappeared. She glared at my outstretched hand and smacked it away like she did back on the ship and got down without my assistance. When we both stood in the waist-deep water, we silently removed our life jackets and flung them over the seat of the jet ski before she turned away from me and started wading a few feet away, staring down at the tropical marine life that swam all around us, not caring that we'd just invaded their territory.

"About fifty yards to your left is a sand bar that's a hot spot for stingrays," I start explaining to her back as she keeps walking, and I quickly move to catch up to her. "A few of the local island resorts have charters that will bring people out to this reef so they can get in the water with them, feed them, and touch them. The stingrays are actually trained now to show up when a tour boat comes in. They know they'll get food, and they act more like happy little puppies than a scary, deadly animal. They'll rub up against your leg, follow you around, and take fish right out of your hand. They continue reproducing right in this spot, year after year and the tourists love it."

I'm rambling about fucking stingrays, but I can't help it. I need to do something to fill the uncomfortable silence so she'll actually look at me and I won't have to apologize to her back. Even though the view from behind her is quite a sight to behold as I watch her bend over to get a closer look at a school of bright red fish that swim around her thighs.

"Did you really bring me out here to discuss the mating patterns of stingrays?" Mackenzie speaks, finally turning around to face me and crossing her arms in front of her.

I ignore the way the motion pushes her tits together and up in her bikini top and keep my eyes on hers instead of trailing down so I don't piss her off more than she already is.

"I'm sorry. I was wrong."

I decide starting with the words Brooke told me to use is the safest bet, slowly moving through the water and closing the distance between us until we're standing a foot apart.

She doesn't make things easy on me, keeping her arms crossed and a blank expression on her face, as she squints from the bright sun shining down above us and looks up at me.

Clearing my throat uncomfortably, I take a deep breath and rip the Band-Aid off, looking down at my feet through the water instead of at her face.

"The other night on the balcony, I decided to ignore all the reasons I shouldn't cross the line with you and give in. The whole time, regardless of how fucking amazing it was, I told myself that would be it. Just that one taste would get you out of my damn system and then I'd be able to go back to work and get my head on straight," I begin, running one hand through my hair nervously, hoping she doesn't try to kick me in the balls. "I should have been open and up front about it with you, and I'm an asshole for not saying anything. When I woke up the next morning and couldn't get you out of my head, knowing there was no way I'd be able to stick to my guns about that being a one-time thing, I started fucking things up with work and it pissed me off. It made me angry and I took that anger out on you in the worst way possible. Pissing you off and pushing you away was easier than admitting the truth."

Taking a breath, I finally look up from my feet and into her eyes. She stares at me quietly for a few minutes before she breaks the silence.

"And what truth was that?" she asks softly.

"That for the first time since I started working on a yacht, I let something distract me from my job. Made me not care if I threw it all away, made me forget about my responsibilities and, as stupid as this sounds, my dreams."

I wait for her to throw her head back and laugh at what a pussy I sound like, but it never happens. She sighs loudly, unfolds her arms in front of her and throws them up in the air in irritation.

"First you insult me by thinking I'm a rich, spoiled princess, and now you do it again by assuming I'm such a horrible person that I'd let you lose your job or throw away whatever dreams you have," she replies, shaking her head at me. "I'm not asking you to marry me and run off into the sunset after a couple of kisses and one orgasm, so turn that inflated ego down a notch."

I can't help but smile at her attitude, wishing it wasn't the cutest fucking thing I'd ever seen.

"For the record, I know you're not a rich, spoiled princess. At least, I know that for a fact now, and I'm sorry for what I said to you."

She curses under her breath and glares at me.

"Fucking Brooke. I knew she'd been up to something after that little smile and wink she gave you back on the boat. Whatever, at least it made you apologize and admit you were a giant asshole."

I didn't exactly admit *that*, but I'm not about to point it out now when she seems to be on her way to forgiving me, and I no longer worry for the safety of my balls.

"I get it, things happening between someone on the crew and a guest are frowned upon, you're not much of a rule breaker and lost your shit when you broke a cardinal one. Well, for your information, I've never let anyone stick his hand down my pants after only two days of knowing him, so I guess we're both clueless on how this is supposed to work," she shrugs.

I let out another sigh of relief even though part of me wants to cheer in victory knowing I'm the only man she's let do something like that to her after only a handful of days.

"So, what do we do now?" I ask.

"Hell if I know. Like I just said, I've never done something like this before. But just so we're clear, regardless of what my former best friend may or may not have told you, I'm not going to tell you my whole life story or about *my* hopes and dreams, and I damn well don't expect you to do it either."

She takes a step closer to me until we're only standing an inch apart and I can feel the heat from her sun-warmed skin right through my swim shirt.

"I accept your apology, but that doesn't mean I still wouldn't get a cheap thrill out of shoving you overboard and watching you drown, so don't piss me off again on this trip," she states, craning her neck to stare up at me.

I can't help but laugh even though every time I'm within touching distance of her, I want to run my hands all over her body and say "to hell" with responsibility and rules. But I made my decision and I need to stick to it. Even if she's forgiven me, and even if I'm dying to touch her again and listen to her come apart in my hands, at least we're now on the same page and she knows where I'm coming from.

"I'll probably kick my own ass later for admitting this, but I've had a lot going on lately and I've been in something of a dry spell. A yearlong dry spell that gets more depressing with each passing day. I'm still pissed at you, but hell, I enjoy angry sex just as much as the next person," she tells me with another easy shrug, making me choke on my laughter and want to come in my pants all at the same time.

"I can't...I just...I thought we were in agreement," I stutter. "I can't jeopardize my job. Not right now."

The corners of her mouth tip up into a smirk and,

Christ, if it isn't the most adorable thing I've ever seen. She's funny, beautiful, sarcastic, defiant and fucking adorable, all rolled into one hot little package. If I wasn't in the process of trying to get my head on straight so I could get back on that ship and concentrate on my job, I'd be in deep shit with this woman.

In a flash, her arm slides around my waist and her hand slides down, grabbing a handful of my ass and tugging me up against her.

"Oh, I heard you," she replies softly, still staring up at me with that cute fucking smirk on her face, making my dick swell in my swim trunks. "And I'm pretty sure *you* heard *me* when I said I wasn't looking for a white picket fence or for you to throw away your hopes and dreams over someone you just met. Don't worry, as long as you stop acting like an asshole, your job will not be in jeopardy."

I swallow thickly and have to grit my teeth as she pushes up on her tiptoes, forcing her body to slide against mine as she moves herself up closer to my height.

"Obviously, I'm an idiot and glutton for punishment, because I still want to fuck you," she whispers against my mouth, making me close my eyes and groan under my breath hearing her talk like that. "And judging by the raging boner I felt against my ass the whole ride here, and the one currently poking into my stomach, I'm pretty sure you feel the same."

With that, she drops the hold she has on my ass and takes a step away from me. When I finally remember how to breathe again, I open my eyes to find her a few feet away, looking back at me over her shoulder.

"Are you coming, or are you just going to stand there staring at my ass until the sun goes down?" she asks sarcastically, making my eyes flash guiltily away from the ass I was just ogling.

Jesus Christ. A dirty mouth and fucking adorable.

If I were a different man, I'd be falling for this woman in record time. It's bad enough she's clearly going to make it impossible to stay away from her for the rest of this trip. At least we're in agreement about this not turning into some stupid happily ever after. Even though I don't know everything about her, I'm pretty confident that she's not the type of woman to turn into a stage five clinger who boils a bunny when it's over.

It's apparent I have lost the battle when it comes to keeping my distance from Mackenzie Armstrong. As long as we both agree I can't fuck up my job anymore and neither one of us does anything stupid to screw that up, maybe it's possible for me to give her that quick vacation fling she needs to take her mind off of things.

I'm nothing if not a giver, and as long as she doesn't mess with my head any more than she already has, and we're on the same page about keeping this light and fun, I'll give her whatever she wants.

For the next couple of days at least.

CHAPTER 14

⚓

Mackenzie

"FEMINISTS ALL OVER the world would be hanging their heads in shame at me right now, wouldn't they? I'm weak and pathetic and easily forgiving of asshole behavior," I complain to Brooke, leaning against the doorframe of our bathroom while I watch her apply make-up. "Tell me I'm weak and pathetic."

Brooke sighs, pulling her face away from the mirror and lowering the mascara wand from her eye to stare at me in the reflection.

"I will do no such thing. You aren't weak and pathetic. And you aren't easily forgiving, either. You stuck to your guns and made him feel like a jerk. What you are, is easily distracted by a pretty face and a magic dick," she informs me, turning around to lean against the sink.

"You're right," I whisper, my eyes widening with this sudden discovery. "I've always rolled my eyes at women in books who keep going back to the same asshole over and over again. It's because of the magic dick. And now I get it."

"The fucking magic dick," Brooke agrees with a nod.

"But seriously, this doesn't make me weak and pathetic that I forgave him so easily and basically threw my vagina at him in a challenge?" I ask as she turns back to face the mirror and finish applying her mascara.

"He explained why he did what he did. He was an assuming asshole, but he still realized he was wrong and fixed it. You accepted his apology and admitted you're still in need of a good dicking, and he's the closest available dick to give you said dicking. I see nothing wrong with that," she shrugs.

"That was a lot of dicks in one sentence."

"There are a lot of dicks on this boat. You think you've got problems? Ben is the best sex I've ever had and he's a man-whore," she complains, shoving her mascara tube back into her make-up bag and grabbing her bottle of perfume from the counter.

"How do you know he's a man-whore?"

"Because he told me," she replies, spraying a cloud of perfume in front of her and then doing the upper body roll to move herself through the mist. "He fucked that quiet, mousy chick Jessica the day before we got here. But *damn* if that man doesn't make my toes curl. Again, I see nothing wrong with what you did. You need a distraction in your life. I can't handle watching you stare at your dad all the time, looking like you're on the verge of puking."

Fine, maybe I'm not a huge moron for still wanting to sleep with Declan, but I'm definitely an idiot for worrying about my behavior with *him* right now instead of sucking it up and going in search of my dad.

As soon as Declan and I got back to the ship and got up to the balcony, he told me he'd see me at dinner, used his finger to make an X over his heart, and promised he was done being an asshole and avoiding me. And in between glances at my father over dinner and trying to get up the nerve to pull him aside, I couldn't stop looking over at Declan as he stood behind the bar, smiling at me whenever we made eye contact.

Brooke puts the cap back on her perfume bottle, sets it down on the counter and walks over to stand in front of me, grabbing both of my hands in hers.

"Mackenzie, we only have a few days left of vacation. Your dad seems relaxed and happy, and while I'm fully on board with him finally finding out the truth about the bitch he married, I don't see any problem with you waiting until we get back home," she tells me softly, giving my hands a reassuring squeeze. "The end result will still be the same whether you do it now, or a week from now. Let him have his few remaining days of peace, and let Mr. Magic Dick give you *his* piece until then."

I yank my hands out of hers when she laughs, smacking her lightly on the arm.

"You're so disgusting."

"And you love me for it," she smiles, moving around me and out into the room. "Besides, without me, Declan never would have seen the error of his ways and apologized. You're welcome."

Following her over to the bed, I watch as she sifts through every article of clothing she dumped on top, looking for something to wear.

"I'm not thanking you for telling Declan my personal business."

She holds up a black, strapless dress to the front of her with a questioning look and I shake my head.

"I didn't tell him everything, just a few important facts so he'd stop judging you," she tells me, throwing the black dress on the floor and picking up a red one. "He didn't need to keep thinking you could buy and sell him a hundred times over. He's the type of man whose ego wouldn't let him get beyond it, even if you *are* hot and he's dying to bend you over the deck railing again."

I roll my eyes at her and nod at the red dress she holds up, her voice muffling as she slides it over her head.

"I gave him a few tiny details to make him eat his words and make him feel like the douchebag he was.

Now everything is back to normal and you can get laid," she says with a smile, smoothing the dress down over her hips and fluffing out her long, blonde hair. "Now, go get yourself all prettied up and get yourself some magic dick. I'd appreciate it if you avoid doing it in our room tonight, since Ben is sneaking up here as soon as he gets done with his shift."

She smacks me on the ass as I turn and head back to the bathroom. I give her the finger over my shoulder and shout a warning at her before closing the door.

"Clean that shit off your bed before he gets here. You are NOT having sex with a self-proclaimed man-whore on my sheets."

A FEW MINUTES later, freshly showered and lathered up with my favorite coconut-scented lotion from Nordstrom, the one and only item I have ever splurged on, I exit the bathroom with a cloud of steam behind me. Despite Brooke's order to "pretty myself up," I left my face clean of make-up, let my hair dry naturally in thick waves around my shoulders, and threw on another pair of tiny cotton shorts and a tank top. Whatever happens after I leave this room, the one thing it isn't is a date or a need for me to impress a guy. If all goes well, it's just sex with a guy who already wants to have sex with me, but just needs a little extra push. Since he loved the matching pair of tiny cotton shorts so much the night he had his hand down them, that's as much effort as I'm willing to make. I'm not the queen of seduction, and I can count on one hand how many men I've slept with, but something about Declan, as infuriating as he can be, gives me a backbone and a pile of confidence I've never had.

As Brooke races back and forth between her bed and the closet, tossing things onto the floor in a mad dash, I answer the door for her when there's a soft knock on it, to find Ben casually leaning against the doorjamb with a smile on his face.

"Good evening, pretty lady," Ben tells me as I laugh and move back out of the way so he can enter the room. He stops right in the middle of it and looks Brooke over from head to toe, whistling when she holds out her arms and does a little spin for him.

Wanting to get out of here as quickly as possible before they start going at it like rabbits with me standing right here, I quickly walk through the door and start pulling it closed behind me when Ben suddenly turns around and calls my name.

"Declan is down in the crew laundry room. Second door on the left once you get through the galley. The rest of the crew is already asleep for the night, locked in their bunks, so don't worry about running into anyone," he tells me with a wink.

I want to be embarrassed that Ben knows exactly where I'm headed, but I'm too happy that now I don't have to wander aimlessly all over the ship and hope he comes to me like the last couple of times.

With a quick thank you to Ben, I close the door and leave them to it, tiptoeing down the hall past my family's bedrooms, quietly moving through the darkened main salon and formal dining room. My heart starts thundering in my chest as I stay on my toes and creep down the stairs to the crew area, poking my head slowly into the galley. When I see nothing but an empty kitchen, I keep moving until I exit through the opposite entrance, stopping when I get to the second door on the left.

Quickly glancing down the hall at all of the closed bedroom doors, I take a deep breath, turn the handle and walk right into the laundry room without knocking. The room is larger than what I thought it was, able to fit six sets of stackable washers and dryers along with a long white counter with a bunch of cabinets under-neath. Half of the counter is stacked with folded sheets and other linens for the ship, and the other half is covered with piles of crew uniforms.

Declan looks up from the dryer, where he's current-ly pulling a load of towels out, when I close the door behind me and lean my back against it to calm my racing heart.

He must have changed out of the white polo and khaki shorts after his bartending duties during dinner ended a few hours ago, and now he's wearing that same pair of worn jeans that drove me crazy the other night. Any second thoughts I'd been having on my way down here are quickly put to rest when I see he didn't throw on another tight, faded t-shirt to go with the jeans this time. Oh, no. Standing across the room with his arm full of fluffy white towels, Declan has decided to forego a shirt altogether.

Sweet mother of God. Is there a stealthy way to wipe drool from your chin?

I knew this guy had some muscles, it was hard to miss them when he kissed me and I had been pressed up against his chest, when I clutched onto his arm as he was giving me an orgasm, and especially with that blue swim shirt he had on all day today. But nothing could have prepared me for Declan with his shirt off.

"J'ai tellement envie de toi…" I trail off as I stare at his hard body, telling him I want him, knowing he likes it when I speak French and hoping it moves him into action.

With his eyes glued to mine, he tosses the towels over to the counter and my eyes immediately take in his chiseled chest, the muscles of his abs as he twists his torso, and the V-shaped indents outlining his midsection that I've only read about in books or seen in movies.

"You're not going to make this easy on me, are you?" he asks in a low, serious voice when he turns back to face me.

"Nope," I reply, my hands still pressed against the door down by my sides to keep me standing upright, so I don't do something stupid like collapse at his feet in a puddle and start praying to the God of hot guys, thanking him for his excellent work.

His eyes remain glued to mine as he takes a few steps towards me and then suddenly stops.

"And you're not going to go back on your word and do something stupid like fall in love with me?" he asks with a straight face.

The tension immediately leaves my body as I laugh.

"Nope, as long as you can do the same."

He finally smiles at me and takes a few more steps until he's right in front of me and I have to tip my head back against the door to look up at him.

"So, we're in agreement? This is just sex. I still have a job to do and neither one of us is going to screw that up?" he questions, raising one eyebrow as he looks down at me.

Hooking my fingers through his belt loops, I tug him forward with a jerk until his body bumps against me, his bare chest pressing against mine as he lifts his arms and presses his hands against the door on either side of my head.

"Correct," I answer with a small nod, remembering why I came down here in the first place and pulling up a little of that confidence he seems to bring out of me. "As long as you taking me back to your room and fucking my brains out doesn't screw anything up."

His eyes darken as they stare down at me and a muscle ticks in his jaw. When he doesn't say anything for a few seconds, I start to wonder if he's changed his mind and will go back to insisting I'm too much of a distraction he can't afford, even though he's exactly the kind of distraction *I* need right now.

Before I can open my mouth and ask him, he slides one of his hands down the wood of the door and the *click* of the lock engaging by my hip sounds like a gunshot over the hum of the washers and dryers in the small room.

He presses his hand against the couple of inches of bare skin at my side where my tank top has risen up, then slowly slides his palm around my body. Resting it against my lower back and adding a little pressure, he brings my hips forward until I can feel how hard he is for me. My eyelids flutter closed when he dips his head down and presses his lips against my year.

"How about we compromise, and I fuck your brains out right here in the laundry room instead?"

CHAPTER 15

⚓

Declan

ANY DOUBTS I'D had about whether or not I was making a smart choice by giving in to temptation and not staying away from Mackenzie were immediately forgotten as soon as I heard the laundry room door open and saw her standing there in front of me.

I don't know how I'd ever found another woman even remotely attractive with all the make-up they'd piled on, or the shit they'd put in their hair, or the extra attention they put into picking out the right outfit. Mackenzie leaning against the door fresh from the shower with her face void of make-up, wearing another pair of those miniscule cotton shorts and a tight tank top that she probably just threw on without giving it a second thought was the hottest thing I'd ever seen in my life.

The way she stared at me with my shirt off came in

a close second, and hearing her tell me to take her back to my bunk and fuck her brains out made me want to go back on my word of not falling in love with her and beg her to never leave me.

Instead of doing something stupid like professing my undying love to a woman I just met, I quickly grab her hips and lift her body up against mine. She wraps her legs around my waist and drapes her arms over my shoulders as I turn and walk her over to the counter.

Taking my eyes off of her long enough to see what I'm doing, I heft her up higher against me with one arm, and use the other to swipe everything off of the counter and onto the floor. Ashley will have a shit fit tomorrow morning that she'll have to wash everything again, but I can't be bothered with that right now.

Gently setting Mackenzie down on the counter in front of me, I push myself between her thighs. Sliding one hand around the back of her neck and through her long tangle of hair, I grip it in my fist and pull her head back, dipping my head down to the side of her neck. Her hands move from my shoulders to grab the back of my head, and she presses me harder against her neck as I nip and lick and suck the skin there, kissing my way down over her collarbone until I get to the swell of her breasts.

Right when I start to slide my tongue over all that soft, full skin, Mackenzie suddenly moves her hands to my shoulders and pushes me away. Before I have time to question what she's doing, as I stare at her with my tongue practically hanging out, panting like a dog, she grabs the hem of her tank top with both hands and quickly yanks it up and over her head, tossing it to the floor. I've been dreaming about these tits since I first saw her. Sneaking glances of them while she was in a bathing suit, jerking off to them after seeing her in said bathing suit, and getting hard every time I thought about the night I made her come out on the balcony and had one of them in my hand.

Nothing prepared me for the sight of Mackenzie sitting on the counter in front of me with her shirt off, her thick hair hanging in tangled waves over her shoulders and the tops of her breasts, the ends curling right above her nipples. Seeing her bare tits, so heavy and round and full, with her rosy pink nipples hardened and waiting for my touch, makes my mouth water.

"Your tits are fucking amazing," I tell her in awe.

"Thanks. I grew them myself," she replies, arching her back and sticking her chest out a little more.

Fucking adorable.

Smiling like an idiot, I slide my hands around her waist and up her spine as I drop my head to one pert nipple.

I'm rewarded with a low moan from Mackenzie as soon as my mouth wraps around the hardened bud, and I suck it deeply into my mouth. Keeping my lips around her nipple, I swirl my tongue around and around it, loving the way she squirms and pushes herself harder against my mouth.

Kissing my way over to her other breast, I give it the same attention, alternating between sucking hard and flicking the tip of my tongue over her nipple. Her cries of pleasure shoot right to my dick, making it strain painfully against the zipper of my jeans as I take one hand from around her back to palm her other breast in my hand.

"Are you wet for me, Mackenzie?" I ask softly, finally pulling my mouth away from her breasts.

"I don't know," she whispers. "Maybe you should find out."

Reaching behind me, I remove one of her legs from around my hips. She lets it drop to the counter and fall open, and I set my hand on her bare thigh, slowly sliding it upwards until my fingers ease under the hem of her shorts.

Our eyes are locked together and I watch her lids start to flutter closed as I run my fingertips back and forth over the edge of the lace underwear she has on underneath.

"Last chance to change your mind," I whisper, her eyes immediately flashing open.

She answers me by wrapping her hands around the back of my head, and bringing my mouth to hers. Her lips part with a moan when I stop teasing her with the tips of my fingers and push them the rest of the way under her shorts until they're met with the smooth, wet skin of her pussy, which is drenched for me. I touch my tongue to hers as I slide one finger easily inside of her tight heat, slowly pumping it in and out of her body as I make the same lazy motions with my tongue in her mouth.

Her hips start rocking against my hand when I drag my finger out of her and move it up to her clit, gently circling it with the pad of my middle finger. She yanks her mouth away, cutting off the kiss to press her forehead against mine as I take my time, drawing out her pleasure and enjoying the little panting sounds she makes as I swirl my finger around her.

I'm so busy enjoying what I'm doing that I don't realize Mackenzie has removed her hands from the back of my head and has slid them between us, until she's already got the button of my jeans undone and my zipper down. Before I can brace myself, her small, warm hand is down my pants and wrapped around my cock in record time.

"Fucking hell," I mutter under my breath when she squeezes me in her hand and starts pumping it up and down my length in the same slow, torturous way that I'm touching her pussy.

I think I hear her mumble something about "magic dick," but I'm probably hearing things considering the washers and dryers are all running and humming around us, and I'm close to forgetting my own name with way she jerks me off better than I've ever done myself.

"Why couldn't you have been an ugly woman with zero personality?" I complain in between groans as she moves her hand down to the base of my cock and then palms my balls.

"I'm going to forget you said that and pretend I'm not offended for women everywhere by that comment, because I'm too distracted by what you're doing with your fingers right now," she tells me with her own moan of pleasure when I thrust two of those fingers inside her.

I pump them hard, in and out, the heel of my palm rubbing against her clit each time I push them back in. I look down between us at my fingers as they disappear in and out of her body, before I quickly pull them all the way back out, and she lets out a protesting whimper.

Grabbing the sides of her shorts with both hands, she lifts her hips for me as I yank them and her lacy underwear off her body and toss them across the room.

"Good, because I plan on erasing everything from your mind right about now," I inform her as she watches me reach into my back pocket and pull out a condom. "I really wanted to drag this out a little longer, but I need to be inside you."

Without another word, she leans forward and pushes my jeans down my hips while I make quick work of tearing open the condom wrapper and sliding it down over my cock. I take a second to appreciate the scene in front of me: Mackenzie sitting on the counter, leaning back on her hands with flushed cheeks and her tits dotted with a few red marks from my sucking, her bare thighs spread open, and her pussy dripping for me.

Wrapping one arm around her, I pull her body closer to the edge of the counter, palm my dick in my free hand and line it up with her entrance. She locks her arms around my shoulders and her legs around my waist, and I hold myself still, pressing my forehead against hers and giving her time to change her mind, even if it might kill me.

Tightening her thighs around me, she pulls me closer until just the tip of my cock starts to slip inside, and I have to grit my teeth to stop myself from slamming the rest of the way into her pussy.

Moving her hands from my shoulders, she clutches her fingers in my hair, forcing my head up to look her in the eyes. Then, she tilts her head to the side of my face and whispers in my ear.

"Fuck me, Declan."

She barely finishes the sentence before I'm pulling my hips back and then thrusting into her, hard and deep. Her hands smack against my back and her fingernails dig into my skin when I don't waste any time, pulling my cock right back out before slamming inside of her again. She's so unbelievably tight and hot that I have no idea how I'm going to last longer than five seconds. I've never felt anything this amazing in my life.

Her pussy grips my cock like a fucking vise; it's so damn good I think I might die from pleasure. My arm tightens around her waist and I brace my other hand on the counter next to her.

"Jesus, Mackenzie, your pussy feels so good," I mumble against her mouth, burying myself to the hilt inside her and then holding still, trying to calm myself down before I come too soon. "You're so fucking tight wrapped around my cock. Touch your pussy for me, baby."

She immediately complies, bringing one of her hands between us and sliding it down between her legs where we're joined. Her arm tightens around my shoulders and I glance down, groaning when I see her circle her clit with two of her fingers.

"Goddamn, that's so fucking hot," I whisper, keeping my eyes down and locked on her fingers as I pull my cock out of her and slowly push it back in.

She moans loudly as I get a leisurely rhythm going, fucking her slowly and watching my cock, glistening with her wetness, pump in and out of her.

Her hips start moving, joining up to meet mine with each push and pull in and out of her body, and her fingers start circling her clit faster. I'm mesmerized by the sight of her pleasuring herself while I fuck her. I can't take my eyes off of her hand between us and her own wetness that's now coating her fingers. I start thrusting my hips faster, fucking her harder, unable to take this slowly anymore.

Each slam of my cock inside her pushes her circling fingers harder against her clit. Her thighs get tighter around my waist and her moans get louder, making my balls tighten, knowing she's close, and thanking God for it. I need to come inside her right now like I need air to breathe, but I need her to come first.

"That's it. Make yourself come on my cock. Let me feel it," I tell her, finally looking up from where she's touching her pussy to see her face.

Her eyes stare right into mine and I feel her fingers graze my cock as she moves them faster and faster over her clit. We're both panting and grunting and moaning and our skin is slick with sweat, neither one of us paying any attention to the buzzing of one of the machines as it goes off from somewhere behind me.

"Oh, God…Oh, God…" Mackenzie suddenly chants, and I pick up the pace, thrusting my hips faster, her ass bucking up and down on the counter with how hard I'm fucking her.

I grit my teeth and almost bite my tongue clean off when I feel her tighten around me and shout my name. It's impossible for me to hold back as her orgasm makes the walls of her pussy clench and pulse around my cock, and I follow quickly behind her, groaning her name and coming inside her harder and faster than I ever have.

My head drops to her shoulder and I stay locked inside her, trying not to feel embarrassed that I couldn't make this last longer. I stop feeling sorry for myself a few minutes later when Mackenzie finally catches her breath and is able to speak, confirming what I thought I'd heard her say earlier.

"That is definitely one magic dick you've got there, sir," she sighs. "Well done."

She pats me on the back and I pull my head up from her shoulder, unable to contain my laughter even as my dick starts to soften inside her.

Yep. Fucking adorable. I'm definitely in trouble.

CHAPTER 16

⚓

Mackenzie

EVEN THOUGH CAPTAIN Michael kept us anchored for an extra day to avoid bad weather, it was impossible to escape the tropical storm that surrounded us. Since it was a light, easy rain, he pulled anchor in the middle of the night last night and got us to St. Croix by morning.

Thankfully, Declan and I had just finished our romp in the laundry room when the captain called for him on the radio to help with the anchor, and I didn't have to worry about that whole distracting him from his work thing.

I haven't been able to stop smiling since he snuck me out of the laundry room, giving me a hard, fast kiss before heading up to the deck to do his job. Not even Allyson and Arianna's shitty moods about being stuck inside the ship could wipe the giddiness off my face.

"What do you mean you're going over to St. Croix? It's, like, raining," Arianna says in disgust, standing in the doorway of my cabin with her hands on her hips, watching me fill up my small, waterproof backpack with a towel and an extra change of clothes.

"It's just rain, Arianna. I'm not going to melt," I tell her with a sigh, zipping the pack closed and sliding one strap over my shoulder.

When I woke up this morning and looked out my cabin window at the overcast sky, knowing Allyson and Arianna wouldn't be caught dead going out in the rain, I quickly came up with a plan to spend the day alone with Declan, not really sure if it would work, but praying it did. I told Brooke my plan, and she passed the idea on to Ben while he worked as bartender in the formal dining room making mimosas for my stepmonsters while we waited for breakfast to be served, who in turn relayed it to Declan who was busy up in the wheelhouse meeting with the captain.

By the time the breakfast dishes were being cleared away, the plan was set.

"I can't believe you're going horseback riding. They're so gross and dirty," Arianna complains with a curl of her lip.

I brush past her and out into the hallway, making sure to smack my shoulder into hers a little more roughly than necessary, smiling to myself when she huffs and calls me a bitch.

Just in case hell froze over and Allyson and Arianna decided to go over to St. Croix, anyway, to get their shopping fix, I added an extra security measure to make sure I would be alone with Declan by booking a horseback riding excursion on the island. Getting wet AND taking a ride on a "gross and dirty" animal were things those two would never do, even if their life depended on it. And even though my dad has started being a little firmer with them in the last few days, there's still no way he'd leave the boat without them.

Now, there was only one last hurdle to overcome, and I kept my fingers crossed as I made my way up to the sundeck where I found Captain Michael, Ben, and Declan waiting for me.

I made sure to smile and greet them all equally, even though I wanted to take a few minutes to stare at Declan. I had to do everything in my power not to blush when I got my first look at him since last night. I couldn't stop thinking about what we did, and each step I took towards the three men brought the delicious soreness between my legs right to the front of my mind as I remembered every second of him fucking me on that counter.

"Good morning, Miss Armstrong, are you sure you still want to go out in the rain today? It's not going to get any worse and it's still pretty warm out, but the rain doesn't look like it will be letting up any time soon," Captain Michael greets me with a nod and a smile.

"I'm sure, Captain, thank you for asking. I'm looking forward to spending a quiet day in the rain on a beautiful island," I reassure him.

"Excellent. Ben will be accompanying you over to the island and make sure you have everything you need, take you wherever you want to go, and keep you safe. St. Croix is a great place with very friendly people, but we always like to make sure our guests don't have any troubles when they leave the ship," he informs me, telling me what Ben already explained would happen when the captain found out I'd want to leave the ship.

Deckhands always escort guests around an island the ship visits, keeping their distance if they want to be alone, but still close by in case anything is needed, and always at the ready to take them back to the ship whenever they want. Since Declan is the Bosun and in charge of the deckhands, he always has to remain back at the ship in case anything happens or the captain needs him, which is the last hurdle we need to overcome.

"Actually, Captain, I forgot to tell you this, but I'm allergic to horses. I'm so sorry I didn't mention this earlier. I know Miss Armstrong had her sights set on going horseback riding today. Maybe she'd like to pick another activity?" he asks, while I try not to smile at how sincere and apologetic he sounds.

"No, no, whatever Miss Armstrong wants is what she gets," Captain Michael tells me with a smile.

"Declan, would you mind taking Ben's place today? I'm sure Ben can handle your duties in your absence."

I try not to jump up and down and squeal when Declan gives me a slow smile before turning to nod at the captain.

"It's no trouble at all. And I'm sure Ben will have no problem staying behind today. I'll have my cell phone on me in case anything comes up," Declan tells him.

And just like that, our plan falls perfectly into place.

"I CAN'T BELIEVE you've never ridden a horse before. Your dad doesn't have a hundred purebred, champion horses locked up in a sprawling stable somewhere?" Declan asks, grabbing my hips and helping me up and onto the beautiful black Arabian I was given.

Once I'm in the saddle, I look down at him in annoyance.

"You're doing it again. Making snap judgments when you don't know anything about me."

He winces, closing his eyes and sighing before opening them back up and looking at me apologetically.

"I'm sorry. I promised I'd stop being an asshole, and you're right. It was wrong of me to assume."

"Can we get that printed on a t-shirt? I've never heard a man say that to me once, let alone twice," I joke as I watch him mount the white horse next to me. "And you're forgiven."

He grabs the reigns, holding them up and showing me how to do it. I copy his motions, gently tapping my heels against my horse's flanks to get him to start walking, just like Declan does.

"I can't believe the owners let us take out horses alone without one of their guides," I muse as we walk our horses slowly, side-by-side, out of the fence and onto the trail that will take us around the island.

"That's one of the many perks of working on a yacht. You get to know the owners of all the excursion companies over the years, and they're willing to do favors for you. Jill and Eric, the owners of the horse farm, retired to St. Croix the year I started working on the *Helios*. They're good people," he explains.

The rain has given us a reprieve for a little while. The air is still hot and the sky is still overcast, but nothing can take away from the beauty of the lush, tropical island as we make our way down the beach, right next to the water.

"I'm really sorry about the comment I made. It's a habit. And one I need to fix," Declan apologizes again as we guide our horses up to a trail that will take us to the rain forest.

"Why do you hate people who have money so much?" I ask, ducking my head when we move under a few low-hanging branches.

"Have you *met* your stepmother and stepsister?" he jokes.

"Point taken," I reply with a laugh. "If it makes you feel any better, I hate them with the burning fire of a thousand suns, and hope they choke on their hair extensions. When you walked in on Marcel and me in the galley the other night and he laughed, I just got finished telling him I couldn't stand those bitches I'm related to."

He throws his head back and laughs, blinding me with his dimples and making me suddenly aware of the rocking motion my hips make in the saddle as the horse eases his way through the forest surrounding us.

"Honestly, a lot of the guests we get aren't that bad. They're laid back and nice. But the rest are like Allyson and Arianna. One, or several dozen, bad apples spoil the bunch and all that bullshit," he tells me with a shrug.

I understand his quick judgment of me a little better now. It doesn't completely erase the hurt his words caused at the time, but at least I don't feel like such a weak woman for accepting his apologies so quickly. I know what it's like to be around Allyson and Arianna all the time, but I can leave whenever I want if I've had enough of their entitled, rude behavior. Declan's job is catering to people like them twenty-four-seven. If he wants a paycheck, he has to suck it up and deal with it. He can't just walk away and pretend like they don't exist.

We ride our horses together in comfortable silence for the next few miles, Declan breaking the quiet peacefulness of the beautiful landscape every so often to point out a landmark or tell me about the history of a specific spot. When we get so deep in the woods that the air becomes heavy and thick and the plants and trees suddenly go from regular green to a color so lush and bright it looks like we're staring at a painting instead of real life, I know immediately that we've made it into the deepest part of the woods and found the rain forest.

Declan pulls back on the reigns to stop his horse and I do the same. We both dismount and he ties his horse to the closest tree before doing the same with mine. Grabbing my hand and interlacing our fingers, he pulls me along the trail, deeper into the trees, until a light, warm mist starts falling around us.

I wore a bathing suit under my sheer cover-up for this trip, so I don't really care if I get wet, and I have a dry change of clothes in my backpack we left back at the horse farm. I close my eyes and tip my head up to the sky, letting Declan lead us wherever he wants to go as I enjoy the feel of the warm, tropical spray on my face.

My eyes fly open when my body is suddenly yanked forward and I slam into Declan, who's staring down at me with a hungry look in his eyes. He wraps his arms around my waist, and I press my hands against the damp material of his t-shirt clinging to his chest.

"You are so fucking beautiful," he says softly, shuffling his feet and moving me backwards until my back bumps into a large tree.

One of his hands comes up between us and he uses the tips of his fingers to brush a few wet strands of hair out of my eyes and off my forehead, before trailing them down my cheek.

My eyelashes are dotted with drops of rain and I blink them away as I stare up at him, the messy spikes of his hair glistening with the mist that is falling down around us. I feel the steady beat of his heart begin thumping faster under my palm, which is still pressed to his chest.

"Are we all alone out here?" I whisper, feeling the heat of his skin under his wet shirt as I slide my hand up his chest and lift it off of him to run it through the thick strands of his wet hair.

"Another perk of my job. This rain forest is on private property. I called the owners while you were meeting your horse and found out there weren't any tours scheduled today. We've got the whole place to ourselves."

I only heard half of what he said since in the middle of his explanation, his hand moved down off my face, over my breast, down my side, and his palm was now running up the inside of my thigh, pushing up the wet material of my cover-up as he goes.

"Whatever will we do with ourselves all alone out here? I'm not sure—"

I let out a small gasp, my head thumping back against the tree behind me and my eyes closing, when he cut off my words by pushing my bikini bottoms to the side and, without any hesitation, plunged two of his fingers inside me.

"Jesus, how are you this wet already?" Declan groans, pumping his fingers in and out of me slowly, adding his thumb to circle around my clit.

"Because of you," I tell him, groaning when he slams his fingers in hard and deep, all the way to his knuckles.

"You're so good for my ego," he says with a smile in his voice as he works me over, fucking me with those expert fingers and kissing the drops of rain off my cheek and moving down to my neck.

"Declan, please," I beg with a whisper, rocking my hips against his hand and wrapping my arms around his shoulders to pull him closer. "I can't...I need..."

I trail off, unable to form words as my legs start to shake as his fingers thrust deeper. I can't hold off the release that is taking over my body, but I want him with me when it happens.

"Let go, Mackenzie. Let me feel you come on my fingers."

I finally open my eyes and shake my head at him, grabbing his cheeks with my hands and bringing his lips to mine.

"J'ai besoin de toi en moi. I need you inside me. Now. Please," I beg again, speaking in French just for him, whispering what it means against his mouth.

"Fuck, you're going to be the death of me," he mutters, quickly pulling his fingers out of me, grabbing a condom out of his back pocket, and shoving his shorts down his hips just enough to free his cock.

Pushing my bikini bottoms down my hips quickly, I let them fall to my feet and kick them away. My heart beats wildly in my chest, and my pussy aches and pulses with the need to come as I stare down between our bodies and watch him put the condom on his thick, hard cock so quickly that his hands are a blur.

He moves with the speed of light, clearly needing me as much as I need him. One of his arms wraps around me and tugs me roughly to him as his eyes stay locked on mine. His free hand grabs my thigh and brings it up around his hip while at the same time he bends his knees and slams his cock up and into me, burying himself deep in one hard thrust.

We both groan in pleasure at the same time. With the warm mist of rain falling down around us and soaking our bodies and the gentle sounds of tropical wildlife echoing through the rain forest, Declan fucks me up against a tree.

It's brutal and it's hard. I know I'll have bruises up and down my spine, and I don't care. I've never been taken like this, out in the open and with such raw abandon. He fucks me like he can't get enough of me, can't get close enough, can't get deep enough. He growls against my lips as he drives his cock in and out of me and it takes my breath away.

He tells me how good my pussy feels, he tells me I'm so tight that it drives him insane. He tells me he never wants to stop fucking me. Dirty, wonderful things that no man has ever said to me before and words I never thought would turn me on so much. Maybe it's because they're coming from Declan. Maybe it's because he makes me forget the world around me and allows me to just enjoy life.

His hips piston between my thighs, his groin smacking against my clit each time he plunges his cock inside me. It doesn't take long for the orgasm that was teetering on the edge when his fingers were inside me to roar back to life and explode out of me.

I scream Declan's name up to the sky and cling tighter to his body as I come and wave after wave of pleasure pulses between my thighs. He thrusts his cock into me a few more times before slamming himself as deep as he can, burying his face into the side of my neck as he curses and mutters my name while he comes inside me.

Neither of us moves for several long minutes as we both catch our breath. My back is still pressed up against the tree, my leg is still flung over Declan's hip, and his cock is still buried inside me as he squeezes his arms around me and holds me to him as tightly as he can...as if he never wants to let me go.

I've always known I was never the type of woman

who could handle a one-night-stand or a quick fling. I threw caution to the wind and gave it a shot with Declan to try and finally have some fun in my life.

Something tells me, as we stand under the canopy of trees, wrapped around each other, that no matter what I tell myself, I'll never be the type of woman who can handle something like this. If I'm not careful, this quick vacation fling will quickly turn into something that could break my heart.

CHAPTER 17

Declan

"*J*ESUS, HOW ARE *you this wet already?*"

"*Because of you...*"

"*Because of you...*"

"*Because of you...*"

"Declan, did you hear me?"

I jerk my eyes away from the window in the bridge when the captain's voice penetrates my thoughts, trying to wipe the guilty look off my face.

"Yes, sorry, sir, I heard you. I was just thinking about the things we needed to get done today while the guests are off the ship.

The lie flies easily off my tongue, and I mentally curse myself that I'm being dishonest with Captain Michael for the first time in four years. I didn't hear a word he said, and I definitely wasn't thinking about what I needed to do around the ship. I was too busy staring down at Mackenzie while she lounged on the couch down below in that damn blue bikini, thinking about what happened in the rain forest yesterday and how completely and utterly fucked I am. I've always been good at keeping emotions and feelings separate from the women I hook up with, but something about Mackenzie makes that impossible. Not only is she the best sex I've ever had, she's fun and easy-going. I find myself wanting to tell her everything, about my life, about my past, and most importantly, about my future. I'm starting to wonder what the hell I'll do with myself when she's not on this ship anymore and it's freaking me the fuck out. It's also distracting me, something we both promised wouldn't happen. I'm not angry, not like before. I'm just…confused. And I don't want the captain thinking my head isn't on straight, especially now, when everything I've ever wanted is right within my grasp.

"I asked if everything was going okay with your studies for the captain's exam," he says, repeating his earlier question that I missed.

"It's going fine, sir. I plan on taking the exam as soon as the charter season is over."

I don't tell him that I haven't even looked at the book since Mackenzie stepped foot on the *Helios*. It's not like I really need to study since I've been preparing myself for this exam for the last two years, but I definitely shouldn't ignore it and just assume I'm going to pass. I need to find a way to balance everything. I have no fucking clue how to do that, when all I can think about is spending as much time with Mackenzie before she leaves. In three days. Just the idea that I only have three more days makes a knot form in my stomach.

"I know you've been busy with this charter; these guests seem to be a little more demanding than others we've had," Captain Michael replies with a chuckle, being professional enough to not come right out and say that Allyson and Arianna are the biggest bitches we've ever had on board. "But whenever you have free time, feel free to ask me any questions, or spend more time up here in the wheelhouse. Whatever you need to pass the exam."

This is what I've been waiting for since I first asked him at the start of this season if he would help me on my road to becoming a captain. It's everything I've ever wanted, but for some reason, it doesn't make me as excited as it should.

"You've got a good head on your shoulders, Declan. You work hard, you get along with everyone, you handle your crew better than any other Bosun who's ever worked for me, and you don't let anything interfere with that."

The serious look he's giving me makes that knot flare up in my stomach all over again, and I have the urge to rub my hand against it to make it go away. If he only knew just how much I was letting things interfere.

"But, you also need to get a life," he finishes, making my eyes widen in shock.

He laughs at the obvious look of surprise on my face and crosses his arms over his chest.

"You're too serious all the time, Declan. I think you'd make a great captain and I would be proud to mentor you, but do you think I got where I am today by doing nothing but eat, breathe, and sleep this job?" he asks. "My wife would kick my ass. You have to know how to live and have a little fun. You have to have a life off this boat or your guests are going to feel it. You can't give them a memorable experience if you have no memories to draw from."

He drops his arms and pushes himself away from the control equipment counter with his hip, walking over to me and resting his hands on my shoulders.

"Yesterday, after you got back to the ship, was the happiest and most laid back I'd seen you in four years, Declan. You need a little more of that in your life, or this job will kill you and you'll grow to hate it."

I don't tell him I was happy and laid back because I, in fact, got laid while I was off the ship. Not because it's the most unprofessional thing in the world to admit to your captain, but because that wasn't the only reason I was in such a good mood. Spending time with Mackenzie, listening to her talk, watching her love every minute of whatever she's doing, even if it was something as simple as a horseback ride or a walk through the woods in the rain...*that's* what made me get back on board with a smile on my face.

Captain gives my shoulders a squeeze before pulling back and walking around me.

"The guests are planning on having a picnic on the beach for breakfast and then doing some sightseeing around the island. I'm putting you on babysitting duty again today, and you can take Ben with you. Eddie can stay back and handle things here," he informs me. "Go have another day learning how to relax before we pull up anchor tonight and start heading back to St. Thomas."

I give him a smile and a nod, unable to believe what the hell just happened. After he leaves, I stand in the same spot he left me for several minutes, trying to collect my thoughts.

The happiness and calm that settled over me is short-lived when I hear an annoying, whiny voice behind me.

"Why are you avoiding me?"

With a sigh, I turn away from the wheelhouse windows to find Ashley standing in the doorway the captain just exited, staring at me with her hands on her hips.

Shit. I promised Zoe I'd talk to Ashley and I forgot all about it.

While I'm busy trying to come up with something to say, Ashley closes the distance between us, wiping the irritation from her face to smile at me as she rests her hands against my chest.

"I know you've been busy with this charter, but that's no reason to ignore me."

I try not to look at her in disgust, even though that's exactly what I'm feeling as I grab her hands and remove them from my chest, taking a step back.

"I'm not ignoring you, Ashley. I've got a job to do on the exterior, and yours is in the interior. It's nothing new that our paths don't cross all that much during a charter," I remind her.

"But we still get breaks and time off and you're never around. It's because of Mackenzie, isn't it?" she asks, flying right back to being irritated so fast that it gives me whiplash.

"Miss Armstrong is a guest on this ship. My free time has nothing to do with her, and it's none of your business, Ashley," I tell her in a low voice, hoping she drops this before I say something I'll regret that will have her running to the captain.

It's bad enough she somehow picked up on my obsession with Mackenzie, even though we've done nothing out in the open and have barely said two words to each other in front of the rest of the crew. I don't need her running to the captain with her suspicions. I'm lying right to her face, but like I just told her, it's none of her business.

"But I want it to be my business! We're so good

together," she tells me, taking a step in my direction as I take yet another step back.

"We weren't together," I argue through clenched teeth, finding it harder and harder to keep my voice down and not yell at her. "We had sex a few times after drinking too much. I told you at the end of the last charter season that it wouldn't happen again. Have I ever given you any indication I wanted more from you?" I ask, not wanting to hurt her feelings even though she's lost her fucking mind, but unable to come with any other way to get my point across.

"You're going to screw everything up," she tells me, shaking her head and glaring at me. "She's not like us. She comes from a completely different world and would never understand you. Not like I do."

She makes another move in my direction and I'm too pissed, my muscles too clenched in anger to move away this time.

"Does she have any idea you're studying to be a captain? Does she even care that she's distracting you from that? I would never get in the way of your dreams like that. We're the same, you and I. We both know what it's like to struggle and to work hard for what we want. She doesn't have the first clue about that. She hasn't worked a day in her life and would just laugh at you and your dreams"

"You don't know anything about her," I growl, realizing my mistake as soon as the words leave my mouth.

Ashley's mouth drops open and her eyes widen, and it occurs to me that all this bullshit she just spewed was a guess and not based on fact, and I just fell right into it.

"I never thought you'd throw everything away for a piece of ass who was out of your league," Ashley whispers with fire in her eyes.

With my hands clenched to my sides so I don't grab her by the shoulders and shake the shit out of her, I lean my head down closer to her face, keeping my voice low and level.

"I'm telling you this for the last time. What I do is none of your fucking business. Move on. Do your job, and I'll do mine."

We stand here staring at each other silently, both of us fuming. Before I can tell her to get the hell away from me and stay away, I'm saved from fucking things up worse than I already have.

"Ashley? We've got everything ready to take over to the beach for the picnic. Jessica and I are just having a hard time finding the picnic baskets," Zoe interrupts from behind her.

I give her a small smile of gratitude over Ashley's shoulder as she turns around to face Zoe and hustles out of the room without a backward glance.

When she's out of earshot and I hear her feet pounding down the stairs to the crew quarters, I let out a huge sigh.

"Thanks for that," I tell Zoe. "I don't know what I would have done if I had one more second alone with that woman."

Zoe laughs, cocking her head and giving me a small smile.

"She's wrong, you know. Mackenzie's not out of your league, and you're not throwing anything away by being with her."

I swallow past the lump in my throat and nod.

"I know."

"Good," she nods as I walk over to join her in the doorway and we both head downstairs together. "Just wanted to make sure you weren't going to do anything else assholish."

She smacks me on the back and we both laugh, even though my world suddenly feels like it's been turned upside down after everything that happened up in that wheelhouse.

The only assholish thing I'm in danger of doing right now is falling for a woman who makes me laugh, forgives me for being a jerk instead of holding a grudge, and makes me want to do what the captain said and get a life outside yachting.

CHAPTER 18

⚓

Mackenzie

BREAKFAST ON THE beach was beautiful. The crew came over and set everything up in the early hours of the morning while we were still asleep. Under a canopy, they set up a long table covered in linens with vases of tropical flowers lined down the center. Marcel outdid himself with all the food, making every type of breakfast dish imaginable so everyone would be happy. Most shockingly of all was that Allyson and Arianna couldn't find one thing to complain about as we all quietly ate our breakfast under the shade of the canopy, looking out at the crystal clear water, making small talk about the weather that had finally cleared up and what our plans were for the day.

I was surprised to see Declan and Ben had joined the crew during our beach picnic, figuring once they helped the stews bring the food over from the boat, they'd go back to the ship and do whatever work needed to be done back there. Instead, both men quietly helped the women set the table, refill our coffees and orange juices, and stood off to the side talking to themselves to give us privacy while we ate. We'd shared a few smiles during that time, and I couldn't help glancing over at Declan every few minutes as the crew packed up the picnic baskets and coolers and started taking everything back to the boat. I loved watching the way the muscles in his arms tightened as he lifted the handle of the cooler and pulled it through the sand, and how good he looked in a pair of aviator sunglasses, and the dimples in his cheeks when he laughed at something Ben said as the two of them walked side-by-side down the beach and away from us.

I was overwhelmed with a feeling of longing for him, wishing I hadn't made plans with Brooke to tour the island, wanting nothing more than to follow him back to the boat. I don't care if he had to work all day, I just wanted to spend more time with him, even if that meant following him around, watching him do his job.

It's pathetic how attached I've become after only a few days.

"How are you doing, sweetie?" my dad asks, pulling my gaze away from Declan as he disappears down the dock off in the distance and back to the ship.

I watch my father get up from his seat at the other end of the table and move to the empty one next to me, realizing we're alone. Looking down the beach in the opposite direction of the dock, I see Allyson and Arianna walking together at the water's edge, and Brooke is a few feet away from them, squatting down and collecting shells in her hand. I was so busy daydreaming about Declan I hadn't even noticed everyone walked away from the table and left my dad and me alone.

"I'm good, dad," I answer him with a smile as turns to face me in his chair.

"You look happy. Relaxed," he answers with his own smile as he reaches over and pats the top of my leg. "You've been looking a little tired and stressed for a while. I was starting to worry about you."

I don't tell him that it's about time he noticed, not wanting to ruin this rare, small moment of alone time between us.

"I know I've been a little distracted lately and I'm sorry about that, Mackenzie. Things are going to change, I promise."

He gives my leg another small pat before swiveling in his chair to stare out at the ocean in front of us. The silence stretches between us as I stare at his profile. The fine line of wrinkles around his eyes and mouth are deeper. His face suddenly looks older than his years, and I couldn't mistake how completely exhausted his voice was when he spoke. It makes me sad, and it makes me wonder if I'm doing the right thing by waiting until we're back home to tell him what I know. It's going to kill him either way, and all I'm doing by holding off is delaying the inevitable. I feel like the worst daughter in the world right now as I stare at the man who raised me and never made me feel like I was lacking a parent. He did the work of both mom and dad and he did it seamlessly and perfectly over the years, until he met Allyson.

I told myself I would wait until our vacation was over because I wanted him to enjoy these last few moments of happiness, but I know that was a lie. I did it for selfish reasons. Because *I* wanted to enjoy myself and enjoy the time I had left with Declan without worrying about the future.

"Dad—"

I say his name softly, my voice cracking with emotion as he turns and gives me a sad smile. I'm ready to blurt it all out, confess what I know and ease my guilty conscience. I've been keeping the truth to myself instead of sharing it with him as soon as I found out, but he shakes his head and stops me.

"No more heavy stuff. We're on vacation and I want you to have fun," he tells me, the sadness on his face quickly replaced with an easy smile. "I spoke to the captain before we came over here for breakfast and told him I wanted to extend our vacation a few more days. Take our time getting back to St. Thomas. Go have fun today. Be young. Hang out with Brooke and that good-looking deckhand you haven't been able to stop staring at all morning. I'll keep your stepmother and stepsister busy."

My cheeks heat in embarrassment, and I look away from him to stare down into the dregs of my coffee cup. I should have known my father would notice how I couldn't keep my eyes off Declan. Growing up, it was like he had eyes in the back of his head, always one step ahead of me and always knowing what I was up to before I even did it, but it's been a while since he noticed *anything* about me. It makes me happy and sad all at the same time. I should be worried my dad seems to know something bad is coming, and he's avoiding it by extending our vacation, but I'm too busy being thrilled with the knowledge that I'll have more time with Declan. More time to be young and have fun, just like my dad suggested. More time to enjoy this tropical oasis and the man who makes my heart skip a beat before our world comes crashing down around us.

Like father, like daughter. We both seem to want to do everything we can to ignore our problems for a little while longer.

Leaning over and giving my dad a kiss on the cheek, I move away from the table and walk through the sand towards Brooke, hoping she can help me come up with a plan for getting Declan to join us.

MUCH TO MY surprise, when I spoke to Brooke after breakfast I found out she'd already formulated a plan without me and had Ben put it in motion. They scheduled a whole bunch of excursions for us on St. Croix and when Ben told the captain, he readily agreed to let Declan come with us.

While my dad took Allyson and Arianna shopping, the four of us spent the day doing everything St. Croix had to offer. Ben and Brooke smartly picked all the things the other two women would never want to do, just in case they decided to join us. We went to Rainbow Beach and snorkeled, we kayaked through Salt River National Park, hiked through Annaly Bay to the Carambola Tide Pools, then finished off our exploration of the island by stopping at the Divi Carina Bay Resort. The only resort on the island with a casino, where I happily proved to everyone just how good I am at blackjack by kicking Brooke's ass every hand we played at the five-dollar table, while Ben and Declan stood behind our chairs and cheered me on.

After winning enough money and Brooke finally admitting defeat, she declared dinner was on me. Using his connections on the island, Declan spoke to the resort owner and got us two rooms to use for an hour where we could all shower and get ready for dinner. Since Brooke started planning for the day before we left the ship for breakfast, she packed both of us a backpack with an extra change of clothes so we didn't have to waste time going back to the ship for anything, Declan and Ben did the same after they cleaned up from breakfast and took everything back to the ship.

After our non-stop fun, but exhausting day around the island, I was happy to see Brooke packed something casual for me to wear and didn't require too much time getting ready. In my favorite pair of short, worn, but cute jean shorts and a teal, form-fitting t-shirt with a wide neck that hung off of one shoulder, I let my hair air dry into long, soft waves. We met the guys in the lobby where they'd already decided on the best place for dinner.

Brooke slipped her arm through the crook of Ben's elbow and they led the way, Declan taking my hand and interlacing his fingers with mine like it was the most natural thing in the world as we followed behind them.

Now, with my stomach full of the best seafood I've ever eaten and nursing my third beer, Declan and I sit side-by-side on the deck of Rhythms Bar and Restaurant, our backs resting against the picnic table behind us, my feet propped up on the railing in front of us. We stare out at the ocean stretched out in front of us, listening to the faded sounds of the live band playing down on the beach under a canopy a few hundred yards away, both of us laughing when we spot our friends amongst the crowd of people. They're lost in their own world dancing to the music together, neither one of them having any sort of coordination or grace as they flail their arms and whip their heads around like lunatics to that "If You Like Piña Coladas" song.

"This was fun. I needed this today," I tell Declan softly, bringing my Corona up to my mouth and taking a sip as I bump my shoulder against his.

Slipping off his flip-flips next to my own that I abandoned as soon as we turned around on the bench seat a little while ago, he props his legs up on the railing next to mine. His thigh brushes against mine when he crosses his legs at the ankles, and I try not to shiver when he transfers his beer to his right hand, swinging his left arm around to rest on the table behind me, his fingers absently playing with a strand of my hair.

When he showered back at the resort, he changed out of his ship uniform, donning a clean pair of slate gray cargo shorts, pairing it with another one of his soft, faded t-shirts, this one white with the *Helios* logo in gray across the wide expanse of his chest. I can still smell the hotel soap on his skin from his shower, and I can't take my eyes off of the muscles in his neck and the bobbing of his Adam's apple as I watch him take a sip of his beer before turning his head to look at me.

"Brooke mentioned you've had a lot on your plate lately the other day when she was handing my ass to me. Everything okay?" Declan asks softly, his gorgeous green eyes filled with concern as they study me.

"No. But it will be. I hope…" I reply, trailing off, wondering what it is about this man that makes me want to spill all of my secrets and tell him everything.

"Let's just say it's been a rough year," I continue with a sigh, knowing I'm supposed to be keeping things between us light and easy and not unloading all of my problems on him.

I know today wasn't a date. I know technically he and Ben had to accompany Brooke and me all around the island because it's their job, but I couldn't stop myself from pretending that it was more, just for a little while. I know the two of us have no future, and once I leave the *Helios* I'll never see him again. Maybe opening up to him makes me a fool, but it's impossible not to share a part of myself with him when the look on his face says he cares, even if I'm imagining it.

"To say I wasn't happy about my father's choice to remarry is an understatement," I admit. "It's not that I expected him to be alone forever, I just thought he'd make a better choice. Things have just gone downhill since then. He doesn't have a lot of time for me, and he's been ignoring problems that have been staring him in the face for months. I'm not really looking forward to going back home, where reality is going to crash in like a bull in a China shop, and he won't be able to ignore things anymore. At work or at home."

"You work for your dad, right?" he asks.

I wait for him to make a snarky comment about how nice it must be to have a cushy job at my father's company, or how easy it must have been to get the job since I'm related to the owner, but it never comes. I almost wish he *would* say something to piss me off, something judgmental and rude. It would make it easier for me to shut my mouth and not share personal things with him. It would make it easier for me to remember this is a vacation fling and not something more.

"Yes. I started working for him right out of college."

Declan pulls his arm back from around my shoulders, brushing my hair out of the way to wrap his hand around the back of my neck, massaging it gently. His hand is warm and his fingers are magical as they work to ease the tension from my body, turning me into a pile of mush until I feel my shoulders droop and I lean into his side.

"You don't sound very happy about that," he replies.

I turn away from the concerned, imploring look on his face to look back out at the ocean and shrug.

"It's not exactly what I wanted out of life. I never planned on going to work for him, and I never thought I'd find myself stuck there almost five years later," I tell him, wishing I didn't sound so sorry for myself.

It's my own fault I'm in this situation. Even though it was initially my father's plea that I don't leave him or the city in search of what I wanted to do for the rest of my life, it was still my choice.

"So, what *do* you want out of life?" Declan asks,

grabbing my now-empty bottle of beer from my hand and trading it for a new one our waitress just brought over.

"Honestly? I have no clue," I tell him with a humorless laugh. "I majored in graphic design and photography, with a minor in business management. I love being creative and artistic, and I guess I get to do that working for my father in the graphic design department, but designing websites and brochures wasn't exactly what I had in mind. Sitting behind a desk all day in an office building, doing all my work on a computer is as boring and mindless as it sounds. It doesn't make me happy, and lately, it's given me zero free time to have a life."

We both take a drink of our fresh beers as Declan continues to massage the back of my neck.

"I think it's rare for people to know what they want to do right out of college, so don't beat yourself up over it. It took me a lot of years, working a lot of miserable jobs before I figured things out," he explains. "I have a younger sister that I needed to help take care of after our parents died. I did what I had to do to pay the bills and keep a roof over our heads until she became an adult, got her own life, and told me she didn't need me to take care of her anymore."

A wave of sadness washes over me hearing Declan say he lost both of his parents, and I can't help looking at him with newfound awe and respect knowing he took care of his sister after they were gone.

"I still take care of her, sending money home to her whenever I can, which pisses her off to no end," he says with a chuckle. "But once I stopped having that weight on my shoulders, I started figuring out what I wanted to do for the rest of my life. I got my first job working on a yacht four years ago, and the rest is history."

Hearing him talk so easily about himself and learning these new things about him is not helping me remember this is just a vacation fling and we're supposed to be keeping things light and easy. I want to know more. I want to know *everything*. I want to ask him all about his past, and I want to know all about his plans for the future. It makes my heart beat faster and my hand shake around the sweating bottle of beer I hold tightly in my grasp. I bring the bottle up to my mouth and drink to avoid asking questions.

"That's all you need to do," he says, looking out at the water with a shrug. "Find what makes you happy and get the life you deserve. Find a guy to settle down with, pop out two-point-five kids and live happily ever after."

His words make my chest tighten and tears start to tickle the back of my eyes, but they're just the reminder I need that I have to stop pretending this is more than what it is. We might have spent a perfect day together like a normal couple, and we've shared a few personal things with each other, but this isn't going to turn into anything serious. We're not a normal couple. We're a vacation fling, period. His life is on a boat traveling the world, taking care of his sister when he can, and mine is back in New York, trying to save my father and his company from ruin, far away from the peaceful tranquility of the Caribbean.

"What about you?" I ask, finally finding my voice and clearing my throat to keep the quiver of sadness out of it. "Now that you've discovered you're a rule-breaker, and you seem to excel at it, what are *you* going to do to be happy and have a life?"

He smiles down at me at the mention of him breaking the rules and my heart gets caught in my throat thinking of how much I'm going to miss that smile when I no longer have it shining down on me.

"I have a life. It's working on a yacht. I don't have time for anything else and it makes me happy enough, although, it was definitely fun breaking the rules with you for a little while," he tells me with an easy wink, dropping his arm from the back of my neck and looking away from me to give Ben and Brooke a wave as they walk over to the stairs of the deck and make their way up to us.

I paste a smile on my face when they join us at the table, ordering another round of drinks while they try to convince us to go back down to the beach with them to dance until it's time to head back to the ship.

After our drinks come, Declan takes my hand and

pulls me down to the beach with Brooke and Ben. He wraps one arm around me, holding his beer bottle in his free hand, and we sway to the music. I remind myself to stop being an idiot and get my head back on straight. I need to get things back to the way they're supposed to be.

This thing with Declan needs to stay light and fun and a way to distract myself from my problems, not make new ones that I'll never be able to fix.

CHAPTER 19

Declan

RESTING MY ARMS across the ledge of the Jacuzzi, I sigh in relief as I tip my head back and close my eyes, letting the hot water ease my tired muscles. After a day spent traipsing all over the island, then busting my ass around the ship doing things Eddie didn't have time to do, I'm exhausted and worn out.

Not only is my body screaming in protest, my head is shouting even louder. I can't remember the last time I'd been on a date, and I definitely never remembered having as much of a good time as I did today with Mackenzie. Just like always, watching her enjoy herself made me forget it wouldn't always be like this; she wouldn't always be here to remind me to have fun and relax. I forgot about the future and her place in my life and opened up to her about my sister and the loss of my parents, something I've only ever done with Ben.

I liked that she did the same and told me things about herself, even though I could tell she was holding back and not telling me everything. I wanted to know more. I wanted to know everything about her and it scared the shit out of me. So much so, I made that stupid comment about her finding a guy to settle down with. Just saying those words made my chest hurt like someone took a sledgehammer to it. After only a week with Mackenzie, it made me sick to my stomach thinking about her with anyone else but me, and that's not something I have any business feeling for a woman who has a life so far removed from my own.

Regardless of whatever problems she has, I realize I'd do anything to fix them, but I know I can't. Even though her dad extended their vacation by a few days and I have more time with her, I can't afford to get any more attached than I already am. We live in different worlds, and I need to remember that. Just because I feel bad she's working a job that doesn't make her happy, she still has a shit-ton of luxuries and opportunities right at her fingertips. She still has a father with more money than God and can get rid of whatever problem she has with the snap of her finger. It doesn't matter that I feel like I know her well enough to know she'd never do something like that, it's the fact that she still *can*. No matter what kind of similarities we have or the connection we share, we still live polar opposite lives. Daydreaming like a pussy about how I could possibly fit into her world, or explore whatever this is between us, after the ship docks back in St. Thomas is pointless.

I know I need to remember all of the things Captain Michael said to me, and I know that in order to be a good captain I need to let go and have a life. I just need to remember that after this trip is over, the life I have and the things I do to relax won't include Mackenzie.

It doesn't help that after getting back to the ship, I had to listen to Ben make all these plans with Brooke for when we leave them in St. Thomas. The man who vowed to never settle down and was perfectly content hopping from one bed to the next, is now talking about flying out to New York to visit Brooke and looking at the calendar on his phone to see when the best times to have her come visit him in Florida would be. I know I shouldn't be jealous, but I can't help it. Mackenzie might have opened up to me today and crossed yet another line we promised not to by doing that, but I find myself wondering why she hasn't said anything about the two of us still keeping in touch. And I'm pissed at myself for wondering why she hasn't said anything, when I just got done reminding myself all the reasons why we can't.

I've never been so tied up and twisted over anyone before. It's making me question my own sanity. How in the hell have I become so addicted to a woman I just met? What is it about her that makes me feel like I'm losing my mind?

Obviously, Ben and Brooke are able to find a way to make things work and I need to just be happy for them. Brooke told me her mother is a kindergarten teacher and her dad works in a factory. Ben's parents both work at a hotel in Florida, his mother as a maid and his father in maintenance. They come from the same background and from the same world. They have more in common than just the loss of parents and a need to find what makes them happy in life. It doesn't matter that it was a lie I when I told Mackenzie yachting makes me happy and it's all I need in life. It doesn't matter I had to stop myself from telling her this past week with her made me happier than yachting has ever made me, and I suddenly want more out of life than traveling the world catering to the rich and famous and going to bed every night alone.

"Is this seat taken?"

As if thinking about the woman made her magically appear, I push back all of my thoughts and worry about right here and right now, instead of what will happen a few days from now.

"I reserved it just for you," I tell Mackenzie with an easy smile, my dick swelling in my swim trunks as I watch her ease her body into the hot water next to me, reminding me this is all we have. Just sex. Just a couple of days of having fun before we both move on with our lives, even though I'm lying to myself all over again by thinking that.

Instead of the blue bikini she usually wears, she's traded it for a red one that's held together with ties on either side of her hips and behind her neck. Her nipples are hard beneath the flimsy material as she sinks down into the water, and I want to do nothing more than untie the strings at the back of her neck and expose her breasts, seeing what they'd look like dripping with water.

"I got a text from my dad a little bit ago that he's staying with Allyson and Arianna at a resort on the island for the night, and Brooke and Ben just kicked me out of our room," she tells me, moving through the water to straddle me, her knees resting on the seat on either side of my thighs.

She runs a wet hand through my hair, her nails lightly scraping against my scalp as she repeats the motion over and over, and I stare up at her face in the soft glow of the lights embedded in the wood around the ledge of the Jacuzzi.

She so beautiful it takes my breath away. It makes me want to throw caution to the wind and just blurt out how I want to see her again after we get back to St. Thomas. Tell her I know it will be difficult since she's in New York and I'm all over the damn place, but maybe we can make it work.

Pulling my arms down into the water without taking my eyes off of her, I run my palms up the outside of her thighs, grabbing her ass with both hands and pulling her down, nestling her right on top of my erection to stop myself from saying something that would ruin the moment. She's quiet for a few minutes as she looks down at me and my heart starts beating faster as I find myself hoping she says it first. Ease my anxiety and let me know she's thinking the same thing I am right now. *I want you more than I've ever wanted anything, this is more than just sex and I don't want it to end.*

"The captain gave the rest of the crew the night off, so they all left the ship to go bar hopping about an hour ago, and he turned in for the night," I tell her, groaning and clutching her ass tighter when she starts rocking her hips, sliding her core back and forth over my cock that's swelling inside my trunks.

"Imagine that. We seem to be all alone. Can you think of anything we could do to pass the time?" she asks, resting her hands on the ledge behind my head, the movement placing her breasts right in front of my face.

Taking a hand off her ass, I bring it up and pull the triangle of material down, uncovering one breast, leaning my head forward and taking her wet, hardened nipple in my mouth. Her hips rock faster over my cock as I swirl my tongue around her. My heart is at war with my head, telling me to take this slow, make it soft and sweet and fucking *mean* something other than a quick lay in a Jacuzzi, and make her say the words I want to hear.

"I've always wanted to have sex in a hot tub. I've been thinking about this all day today, and here you are, ready to make my fantasies come true," Mackenzie moans when I rub my thumb back and forth over her nipple.

Our day away from the ship and the things we shared with each other don't seem to have her questioning what's happening between us one bit, and I can feel my anger start to rise as she closes her eyes and tips her head back above me. She's still perfectly fine with the fact that sex is all we have, and I try to push the anger back down and feel relieved. I don't need the hassle, and I damn sure don't need to be sitting here, wanting something more from a woman who doesn't feel the same.

Her words are just the thing I needed to tell my heart to shut the fuck up. This doesn't mean anything and it's just about sex. I spent the day stupidly thinking about her becoming part of my future, and she spent the day thinking about being fucked in a hot tub. If that's what she wants from me, that's what I'll give her.

Pushing off the bottom of the tub with my feet, I lift us up and out of the water, turning her body away from mine as I go.

"What are you doing?" Mackenzie asks in confusion as I pull her back down in the water in front of me, setting her feet down on the bottom of the Jacuzzi.

With my hands on her hips, I push my chest against her back, walking us over to the opposite side of the Jacuzzi. Reaching around her body, I grab her hands and set them down on the ledge, telling her not to move as I quickly plunge my hands under the water. I make quick work of her bikini bottoms, yanking the strings on either side of her hips until the red material floats away from her and down to the floor of the Jacuzzi, and I shove my swim trunks down just enough to pull my cock out.

Stroking myself under the water behind her with one hand, I grab her hip with the other and roughly pull her ass back to me, nudging her foot with mine to get her to spread her legs. When her ass is peeking out of the top of the water and her legs are open for me, I bend my knees and line the tip of my cock up with her opening.

"I'm giving you what you want," I finally reply to Mackenzie's question once I have her where I want her, pushing just the tip of my cock inside her. "I'm fucking you in a hot tub."

I punctuate my words by burying myself inside her from behind in one hard thrust, my fingers digging into her hips to hold her in place. Even through the water, I can feel her wetness coating my cock, the heat from her pussy rivaling that of the ninety-degree tub we're standing in. Her body telling me this is what she wants, what she *only* wants from me.

Mackenzie lets out a loud gasp when I fill her, and her head tips forward between her shoulders, her arms still outstretched and her hands still holding onto the ledge in front of her. Without giving her a chance to catch her breath, I pull my hips back and I slam into her again and again, fucking her so hard and fast that the water starts churning and splashing up around us. Without breaking rhythm, I lean around her body and smack my palm against the button that will start up the jets. They sputter and roar to life with a loud hum as I continue punishing her with my cock. Even though I'm pissed at myself for forgetting what this is between us, I can't deny how fucking good it feels to be inside of Mackenzie. How tightly her pussy grips my cock each time I pull out of her, and how her soft whimpers and moans of pleasure tell me she loves what I'm doing to her.

"Je mens. Je suis fou de toi. J'ai besoin de toi," she whispers in rapid French.

I hate the way those words, even though I have no fucking clue what they mean, turn me on even more and make me want to stay buried inside her forever.

I'm pissed and I'm taking my emotions out with angry sex, but I'm still not a complete asshole. I still need her to feel good, and I still want her to enjoy every minute of this if it's all I have to give her. Slowing down my thrusts until I'm just barely sliding my cock in and out of her, I wrap one arm around her waist and hold her tightly to my chest. I lift her body with me as I move until I'm standing up and no longer have to bend my knees to be inside her, never breaking our connection between her thighs.

"Rest your knees on the ledge," I tell her as I slide my hand up her spine and push her body forward until she's leaning over the edge of the tub.

Her knees float up to the small armrest above the seat under the water and she looks back at me over her shoulder as I start pumping in and out of her again.

"Why'd you move—Oh, holy shit…" she mumbles, turning her face away from me to tip her head back, cutting off her own question when I grab onto both her hips and inch her slightly to the left.

I can't help but smirk as she smacks one hand down on the edge of the tub and starts mumbling incoherently, pushing aside the last of my negative thoughts as I give her what she wants.

CHAPTER 20

⚓

Mackenzie

I DON'T WANT *this to end. I want you more than I've ever wanted anyone in my life, but I need more. I need all of you.*

The words were on the tip of my tongue when I sank down into the Jacuzzi next to Declan, but I couldn't bring myself to say them. All I could think about was what he said to me at Rhythms earlier and how he'd laugh at me if I told him that after a week, I knew I was falling for him and didn't care how much it hurt when I finally crashed.

I made myself forget about how good it felt to talk to him and share things about my life with him. I made myself forget how much I enjoyed spending time with him and learning things about his life. I made myself stop wanting more, knowing I could never have it. I forced myself to remember this is just about sex, and I crawled onto his lap and put those thoughts into motion.

Declan seemed more than eager to put us back on the same page, but something felt different about him when he suddenly got up from the seat of the Jacuzzi.

I watched his features turn hard and a muscle tick in his jaw before he swung me around and away from him and pushed me up against the other side of the tub.

I wanted to ask him what was wrong, I wanted to tell him to slow down and that we didn't always have to fuck like our life depended on it, but I couldn't remember how to speak when he ripped my bikini bottoms off and slammed himself inside me. As much as I wanted this to be more than just about sex, as much as I wanted *him* to want more, there was no denying that we were good at this together. There was no denying how much I wanted him or how much it turned me on when he took charge and got demanding. I somehow managed to find my voice and I told him I was lying, that I was falling for him and I needed him. But I took the coward's way out and said it to him in French.

I stopped thinking I was a coward and didn't have to make myself forget about anything when he told me to put my knees up on the armrest and then shifted me to the side. As soon as I figured out why Declan moved me a few inches to our left, I forgot my own name and my hand smacked down on the ledge.

The rush of water from the jet in the wall of the Jacuzzi between my thighs, where Declan so expertly placed me, surges against my clit as he starts moving behind me again, sliding his cock slowly in and out of me.

His fingers dig into my hips as he yanks me back against him, my ass slamming into his groin each time he pulls me back onto his thick, hard cock. My entire body ignites, my skin getting hotter from what he's doing to me than from the water in the Jacuzzi. My arms shake with how hard I'm holding onto the ledge around the hot tub, using it to keep myself upright while I jerk my hips back to meet him.

Each time he fucks into me, it moves the lower half of my body closer to the spray of the jet. Back and forth, back and forth, the rush of the water teases my clit, hitting it hard and then fading away until he thrusts into me again. Even through the hot water of the tub, I can feel myself getting wetter, his cock almost slipping out of me each time he pulls his hips back before slamming into me.

"Does it feel good getting fucked in a hot tub?" Declan asks from behind me, the water splashing all around us as he picks up his pace and my hands start slipping on the ledge.

He sounds angry and, again, I want to ask him what's wrong, but I can't do anything aside from moan loudly when he suddenly stops thrusting, his cock buried as deep as it can be inside me, his firm grasp on my hips holding my body in place.

The spray from the jet no longer has a chance to fade since he stopped moving, and the full force of it stays on my clit, making me a mindless ball of need as I whimper and moan and chant Declan's name.

I arch my back, taking him even deeper as I swivel my hips around his cock that fills me so fully, closing my eyes and reveling in the sounds of Declan groaning in pleasure at what I'm doing.

His hands finally let go of the punishing hold they have on my hips to slide around to the front of my body, making him lean forward and press his chest against my back. He starts rocking in and out of me again, slowly pulling his cock almost all the way out before easing it back in each time, as his palms rest on my stomach for a few seconds before moving down beneath the water.

He fucks me gently, and with his arms wrapped around my body and his hands gliding over my sex, he uses the tips of his fingers to spread the lips of my pussy until there's no barrier between me and the spray of the jet. I try to wriggle away, it's too much, hitting just the right spot in just the right way that I won't be able to stop myself from screaming so loudly everyone on the island will hear me, but Declan tightens his arms around my body and won't let me move.

"Go ahead and scream my name," Declan whispers against the side of my neck, reading my mind. "Let go and let me feel that sweet pussy come on my cock."

He holds me open even wider with his fingers, and lazily pumps in and out of me until I feel myself clench around him and my orgasm hits me fast and hard. It washes over me; making me pulse and throb and, yes, scream his name up into the sky.

"Goddammit, you feel so good when you come," he mutters, his hips starting to thrust faster and harder.

His arms stay locked around me and his fingers stay down between my legs as he moves, and before I know it, the spray from the jets and the feel of Declan driving into me harder, racing towards his own release, makes a second orgasm come rushing up to meet me, making my toes curl and my throat grow hoarse as I continue shouting and moaning through the pleasure.

"Fuck…oh, fuck…Mackenzie," Declan chants, whispering my name when he follows right behind me, slamming into me one last time and holding still as he comes inside me.

His hips jerk slightly with the aftershocks of his orgasm as his body follows mine down, me sprawling over the ledge around the tub and him sprawling over top of me. I can feel his cock pulse and twitch inside me and he groans loudly into my ear when I clench my muscles around him, milking him and prolonging his pleasure.

I can feel the rapid beat of his heart against my back. His body shakes with a chuckle when I smack my hand against the button for the jets to turn them off.

I'm content and I'm sated. It feels like nothing could ruin this moment as we stay locked together in a tangle of legs and arms over the edge of the Jacuzzi, trying to catch our breaths.

We're good together, dammit. Sure, I'm telling myself this after the man just gave me multiple orgasms, but I can't ignore everything else. I can't pretend like this is just about sex when all I want to do is turn around in his arms, snuggle up against him, and do whatever I can to make him smile and laugh again because I can't get enough of it.

I don't care if he laughs at me and I don't care if he thinks I'm crazy. I know I'm screwing up one part of my life by keeping my mouth shut with my father, I'm not about to mess up everything else by keeping it shut with Declan. I don't want to pretend anymore. I don't want to try and be someone I'm not—a woman who can have sex with someone and not develop feelings for him.

"I had to turn those things off before they killed me," I sigh, turning my head to rest my cheek on my arm on the side of the Jacuzzi.

I can't wipe the smile off my face or the nervous flap of butterflies in my stomach when I feel Declan chuckle softly behind me, and he brushes my hair off my shoulder to press his lips there.

The rumble of Declan's laughter suddenly stops, and he pulls himself out of me and scrambles away so quickly that the noisy splash of the water makes me jerk my body up and turn to face him.

"Shit! Shit, fuck, Goddammit," he curses, running one hand through his hair in irritation before he yanks up his swim trunks and fumbles with the tie on the waistband.

"What's wrong?" I ask, using my toes to scoop up my discarded bikini bottoms from the floor of the tub and kick them up to my hands.

"I didn't use a fucking condom, that's what's wrong!" he shouts, finally looking up at me with anger raging through his eyes before he smacks one hand down on the surface of the water and shouts another curse.

I want to tell him it's fine and that I'm on the pill, or make some kind of joke about how I don't have any kind of incurable diseases and hope he doesn't either, just to get him to laugh again and make everything go back to the peaceful, happiness of just a few seconds ago, but the next words out of his mouth make me clamp mine shut as tightly as possible.

"That's just what I need. For a fucking vacation fling to screw up my life."

With that, he turns away from me, stomps across the Jacuzzi to the other side, and pulls himself out, yanking a towel off of the table next to the tub and taking it with him as he walks away from me.

CHAPTER 21

⚓

Declan

"I THOUGHT YOU were finished being an asshole?" Ben asks as we stand side-by-side on the deck, using squeegees to clean all of the windows.

He knew something was wrong when he found me slamming things around the supply closet this morning and wouldn't let it go until I told him what happened last night in the Jacuzzi.

"I was. I AM," I insist, wiping the excess cleaning solution off of the rubber tip before bringing it up above me and pressing it against the window, dragging it down slowly. "I freaked out and I said something stupid, that's it. I'll apologize and it will be fine."

I don't believe the words even as I say them to Ben. Yes, for about one second I had a minor meltdown that I forgot to use a condom, but it disappeared in an instant and I started to get happy about the idea of what could happen. That's what pissed me off and made me say something stupid. My forgetfulness and just how *right* it felt to be inside Mackenzie without there being any barrier between us reminded me she didn't want something more. Anything that happened because of it would be a mistake and it would make her feel trapped. Like she had to stay in touch with me after this vacation of hers is over.

"I get it. Nobody needs to be knocking anybody up they just met. And kids are awful. Nobody wants them, even if they say they do. But something tells me an apology isn't going to cut it this time, and there's more shit you aren't telling me," Ben says, tossing his squeegee into the bucket down by our feet and leaning his shoulder against the window.

I clench my teeth and refuse to look at him, cleaning the window faster so I can get away from Ben's prying eyes.

"Holy shit. You're in love with her," Ben whispers.

The squeegee falls from my hand and clatters to the deck.

"I'm not in love with her. I just met her," I argue, squatting down to grab the tool.

He yanks it out of my hand when I stand back up and tosses it into the bucket with his.

"Fine. Maybe you're not fully in love with her, but you're getting there. So what the fuck is the problem? Maybe you knocked her up, maybe you didn't. Who cares? You two can ride off into the sunset and live happily ever after," he says with a laugh.

"The problem is that she doesn't feel the same!" I shout, regretting the words as soon as they leave my mouth when I see his smile and laughter turn into a look of pity.

"Um, have you asked her if she feels the same? Because, you know, you're not exactly very forthcoming with your feelings, and maybe she's the same way. Maybe—"

"She doesn't," I cut him off, reaching down to grab the bucket and walk away from him. "Can we stop talking about this now?"

Ben runs to catch up with me and follows behind me as I move inside the ship and downstairs to the galley, sticking the bucket in the sink to rinse it out.

"I'm just saying, a little talking goes a long way. Women like it when you open up to them and share shit with them. Stop being so damn closed off and maybe she'll change her mind."

Turning off the water in the sink, I glare at him.

"Since when did you become a fucking love doctor?" I ask.

"I know, right? It's making me a little uncomfortable right now, but I can't help it. Brooke makes me happy, and I want everyone to be happy. Even your sorry ass," Ben laughs.

"Stop being a dumb little shit," Marcel says in accented English, making Ben and I both jump when he suddenly appears behind us in the galley.

"You speak English?" Ben asks in astonishment.

"You're both dumb little shits, but you're the dumbest," Marcel tells me, jabbing a finger into my chest. "You like her, she likes you, stop being—"

"A dumb little shit, I got it," I interrupt, smacking his finger away from me.

"She's not like other women we see on this ship. She's kind and she's funny and she doesn't flash her money all over the place. And for some reason, she's decided to set her sights on *you*. Maybe she feels the same, maybe she doesn't. You won't know unless you try. Pull your head out of your dumb shit ass and give her a reason to feel the same," Marcel finishes, turning his back on me to start chopping vegetables on the island in the middle of the room.

Taking Marcel's words to heart since it's the most he's ever said to me in four years, and there must be a reason he said them to me instead of just shouting at me in French, Ben and I leave the galley and head down the hall to our bunks.

"You're going to give her a reason, aren't you?" Ben asks as he pauses in front of his door and looks over at me.

"I don't know what the fuck I'm going to do, but I should probably at least get the apology part over with first," I tell him with a shrug.

"Excellent plan. You can't exactly convince a woman to fall in love with you if she wants to slit your throat. Good luck with that," Ben says, saluting me before disappearing into his room.

STANDING IN THE doorway of the wheelhouse, I take a minute to stare silently at Mackenzie before she knows I'm here. After dinner, when the captain went to his room to rest, I had Ben tell Mackenzie that Captain Michael wanted to talk to her up here. I knew she'd never agree to come up here if she knew I was the one who wanted to talk to her.

I still have no fucking idea what I'm doing, but watching her with her hands resting on the counter in front of her, staring out at the water with nothing but the glow of the control board lights on her face, makes me want to say whatever it takes to get her to change her mind about this thing between us.

She's still wearing a casual, floral print sundress that she must have had on for dinner. Her hair falls around her shoulders in thick, loose curls. The dress ties up around her neck, leaving her back completely bare, and the short skirt shows off her gorgeous long legs. She's absolutely stunning, and I can't take my eyes off of her. I want to get down on my knees and beg her to stay, but I know I can't do that. What I can do, is give her a little more of myself, let her see who I really am, and hope that it's enough to make her want more.

"I'm sorry."

Her eyes close and her head drops down in front of her when I speak, but she doesn't turn around.

Walking further into the room, I want to move next to her, but I know she'll likely punch me if I do that right now. Instead, I move to stand behind the ship wheel in the center of the room, resting my hands on top of the cold, shiny metal as I stare at the back of her head.

"I seem to always be apologizing to you," I mutter, which finally brings her head up.

She quickly turns around to face me, crossing her arms in front of her.

"You wouldn't always have to apologize to me if you didn't do stupid shit in the first place," she fires back, making a smile tug at the corner of my mouth.

I clutch onto two of the wheel handles harder to stop myself from moving out from behind it and wrapping my arms around her. I want to drag my palms down the soft skin of her back, and I want to bury my nose in the side of her neck and breathe in her coconut smell.

"You're right. I was wrong. And I'm sorry. Again."

I watch her fight with her own smile until she rolls her eyes and shakes her head at me.

"I really need to get that on a t-shirt."

We continue staring at each other in the dimly lit

room until she finally sighs and breaks the silence.

"I'm on the pill and I'm clean, for your information. But you would have known these things last night if you hadn't stormed off like a child," she admonishes me.

"I'm clean too, in case you were worried about that. You're the only woman who's ever made me lose my mind so much that I forgot to protect her," I admit.

"Good to know there won't be anything screwing up our lives from this *vacation fling*," she says sarcastically, throwing my words from last night right back at me and making me feel like an even bigger asshole.

My palms start to sweat around the wheel handles when I realize she stressed the word "vacation fling," and it suddenly hits me how angry she is with me. And not just because I said something stupid and uncalled for last night, but because of *what* I said. I could see the hurt written all over her face when she said the words "vacation fling," and it's still there, shining brightly in her eyes with unshed tears that she quickly tries to blink away.

Have I missed what was staring me right in the face this entire time? I got angry when I heard the words she said in the Jacuzzi last night when maybe I should have been paying more attention to *her*. The way she looked at me and the way she trusted me with her body and small pieces of her life she shared with me. I've been holding back from her because I thought she didn't feel the same, when I should have been pushing forward, opening up and telling her everything.

"Did you know the wheels on ships nowadays are just here for show? They aren't used to actually steer it or anything," I tell her softly, easing my way into opening up to her.

She pushes away from the control panel and closes the distance between us, resting her hands in between mine on opposite spokes of the wheel.

"That seems kind of sad. I like the idea of picturing a captain standing in his uniform behind the wheel of a ship. It's much more romantic that way. Like Titanic, but not so horrifying and tragic."

I laugh, rocking the wheel slightly while her hands continue holding on.

"I mean, it's still fully functional, but the captain only uses it in case of an emergency and the computer system shuts down. So, if we have a massive power failure, you'll still get your romance, minus the tragedy," I tell her.

Our eyes stay locked together as I keep gently moving the wheel from one side to the other.

"You look good standing there behind the wheel," she tells me quietly.

I swallow thickly, taking the opportunity she's giving me, but nervous as hell about what she'll say or think. Her opinion suddenly matters to me more than anyone else in the world. I want to be good enough for her. I want her to see that I want more out of life than cleaning up other people's messes.

"This is all I've ever wanted. To be a captain," I admit quietly, looking away from her to stare down at our hands in case I see something on her face that makes me lose my nerve. "That's why I was so shitty with you when we first met and why I didn't want to cross the line with you. I was afraid of losing my job and losing my opportunity to make my dream come true. I've been studying for my captain's exam for years, putting my personal life on hold and working my ass off, and I'm finally ready to take the test once this charter season is over."

She grabs on tighter to the wheel, forcing me to stop moving it and look up at her.

"I think you'll make an amazing captain," she tells me with a smile and a cock of her head. "You're smart, and you're incredibly anal when it comes to organization and following rules. Sometimes."

She raises one eyebrow as she looks pointedly at me, and I can't help but laugh as she continues.

"Everyone on this boat respects you. I see it every time you talk to them, or every time they come to you with a question or need advice. They look up to you. You're going to pass that test with flying colors and be the best captain in the world."

Mackenzie doesn't even question what I've told her. She doesn't tell me it will be hard and she doesn't tell me it's crazy. She immediately believes in me, and it makes me feel like I can do anything, as long as she keeps looking at me the way she is right now. Like nothing makes her happier than the fact that I've just shared the biggest part of myself with her.

"I'm jealous you know exactly what you want out of life, when I don't have a clue," she tells me.

"I *thought* I knew exactly what I wanted out of life. I had one plan, one dream I wouldn't let anything get in the way of. I never thought I'd stray from it. I never thought anything would make me *want* to stray from it," I admit. "You make me want to break all the rules, Mackenzie. You make me want to change all of my plans."

I watch her mouth drop open with a small gasp, but I keep going.

"Life is crazy as hell. Right when you think you have things all figured out, a storm comes along and throws you off course. You'll figure out what you want and you'll make it happen, because you're smart and strong and fierce."

I finally let go of the wheel and move around it to stand in front of her, needing to touch her so badly it hurts. Cupping her face in my hands, I tilt it up so I can see her eyes and watch them fill again with tears.

"What are we doing?" she whispers. "This is supposed to be light and easy and fun. We're not supposed to be talking about hopes and dreams."

Leaning my forehead against hers, I rub my thumbs

back and forth across the smooth skin of her cheeks.

"We can still keep it light and easy and fun, if that's what's you want."

I hold my breath as she moves her body closer to mine, resting her hands on my hips.

"There are things going on in my life back home. Things I can't—"

I cut off her words with a soft kiss. Just a touch of my lips to hers, holding them there and savoring their warmth and fullness before pulling my head back to look at her.

"We still have a few days to figure things out. If light and easy is what you want, that's fine with me. For now."

She smiles up at me and I slide my hands down over the sides of her neck, her shoulders and her arms, before sliding them around her waist and pulling her against me, feeling a little more hopeful than I did when I first walked in here. I can tell she's still holding back. There's something she wants to tell me, but she's scared and not ready yet. I can work with that. I can wait until she's ready.

"You know, I've been slacking with my studies lately. I could really use a study partner," I tell her.

She pushes up on her toes and gives me a quick kiss.

"I'm an excellent study partner. How about you go get your books and meet me in my room. I might be able to come up with a few incentives to help," she tells me with a wink.

The tension is gone from Mackenzie's face as she teases me, grabbing my hand and pulling me out of the room. I'll let her keep things light and easy for now, give her more of myself in the process, and show her she can trust me.

She can trust *us* and whatever is happening between us.

CHAPTER 22

⚓

Mackenzie

ECLAN'S WORDS FROM last night have been playing in my head ever since we parted in the middle of the night. As soon as he said them to me, I knew there was no way my heart would survive this. I wanted to tell him everything I was feeling, everything going on in my life, but something held me back. The ticking of the clock winding down our time together stopped me from telling him I didn't want to ever leave this boat, or him. Knowing I make him want to change his plans and everything he's worked so hard for scares the hell out of me.

I wanted to be here when he took his exam, and I wanted to be the first one to congratulate him when he passed. I wanted to watch him standing behind the wheel of a ship in his captain's uniform, humoring me by pretending to steer it.

Instead of telling him all of these things, I showed him the only way I could. I kept things light and easy, even though I wanted nothing more than to make them heavy and difficult. My heart soared when he told me I made him want to change his plans, but that's exactly why I had to keep things simple. There's no way I would do anything to prevent him from making his dreams come true. He had his whole life figured out, and mine was a mess. I couldn't bring him down with me when he had everything he'd ever wanted right within his grasp.

After we left the wheelhouse, I made him go back to his room and grab whatever study materials he had, meeting me back in my room where we kicked out Brooke and Ben. We sat in the middle of my bed and I fired off questions, keeping with the whole light and easy theme by telling him I'd take off an item of clothing for each one he got right.

Since I only had on a dress, a bra, and underwear, and he clearly knew all of the material forwards and backwards, it only took three seconds for me to be completely naked. He played along with my plan, not bringing up anything heavy between us. I upped the ante as I sat in front of him not wearing a stitch of clothing. He seemed to be quite pleased with himself, unable to wipe the smirk from his face.

For every question he got right, he had to do whatever I asked. It started out simple with a few kisses, making him remove all of *his* clothes, and a quick back massage while I laid on my stomach and he straddled my body as I searched through the pile of books trying to find the hardest questions I could. It didn't matter. He got every single question right.

I quickly realized it was to my benefit that he answered them correctly. I was so worked up sitting across from him and only having his hands on me every couple of seconds in between questions that I finished off our study session by asking him, "What's the name of that thing you drop to keep a boat in place?"

He grabbed my ankles and yanked me closer to him on the bed, got up on his knees and muttered "Anchor. No more questions," before giving me my reward and putting his head between my thighs.

It was fun and it was easy and it was exactly what I thought I needed until the sun came crashing through my window this morning and I realized I was one day closer to saying good-bye to him.

I wanted to get up and find him and tell him all of my problems with my father and his company. Unload everything on him so I didn't have to carry it around inside me eating away at me. I wanted to make him understand why I'm holding back and not giving him everything.

This is exactly why I pull the covers up tighter around me and burrow deeper into them. I know after the things he told me last night that he'd want to help me. He'd put his life on hold. He'd change his plans so completely for me, forgetting about everything he'd worked so hard to achieve, and I couldn't let him do that.

I hear a soft knock on my door and mumble to Brooke to answer it since I'm sure it's Ben sneaking down here to get a little morning action. When she doesn't reply, I pull the covers off my head and see that her bed is empty.

Flinging the covers the rest of the way off, I get out of bed and quickly throw a short, silk robe over my tank top and shorts before answering the door.

"We need to talk."

My dad brushes past me into the room, not making eye contact as he enters. I close the door and turn to find him pacing back and forth at the foot of my bed.

"Dad, what's—"

"How could you keep this from me?!" He cuts me off with a shout, halting his pacing to throw his hands in the air, staring at me with a mix of anger and irritation.

He's never looked at me like this before, and a flutter of nerves ricochet around in my stomach as I stand completely still by the door, unable to move.

"I knew something was wrong, but I thought it was just the usual stress at work and you having a hard time with me getting remarried and not getting along with Allyson and Arianna," he tells me with a huff of annoyance. "That's why I went along with this vacation idea of Allyson's. She thought it would be a good way for everyone to bond and relax."

He starts pacing again, running his hand through his hair until the neatly styled, salt and pepper strands are sticking up all over the place, and still, all I can do is stand here staring at him. I've been worrying myself sick about how I was going to tell my dad what I'd found out, and I should be relieved I don't have to think about it anymore. I should be happy he somehow found out on his own, but I'm not. All of the worry, all of the stress, all of the sadness I've been feeling, it's written all over my dad's face right now and I feel horrible.

Until he opens his mouth again.

"How could you keep this from me?!" He yells. "All these months you knew, and you didn't say one word!"

I immediately stop feeling sorry for myself and let my anger take over.

"Are you kidding me right now?!" I shout back, moving across the room until I'm standing right in front of him. "I DID try to tell you. FOR MONTHS. I told you there were numbers that weren't adding up. I told you to stop avoiding meetings with the accountants. I told you to pay attention, but you didn't listen! You brushed me off, told me things would work themselves out. Told me I needed to try harder to get along with my stepmother. Yes, I finally got proof a few days into this trip that my suspicions about Allyson were correct, and yes, I decided to let you have your peace for the rest of our vacation until I shared it with you and broke your heart, but don't you dare stand here and put the blame on me."

I watch my father's anger quickly fade, turning into sadness and remorse, but now that I've started, I can't stop. Now that I've found my voice, I can't keep it quiet.

"I put my life on hold the last six months for you, and you didn't even notice. I didn't eat; I barely slept. I handled all of the meetings and phone calls with the board and the accountants. Hell, I even stopped taking a salary! I did everything I could to protect you and help you and YOU DIDN'T EVEN NOTICE!" I scream, my eyes filling with tears. "You didn't even care."

He quickly closes the distance between us, wrapping his arms around me and pulling me to him.

"I'm sorry. I'm so sorry, Mackenzie. I *did* care, I *did* notice. I just...I just didn't want to accept it. I didn't want to believe it. I thought if I ignored the problems, they'd just go away. I'm so sorry you had to deal with this on your own."

I sniffle, pushing out of his arms to swipe away the tears that have fallen down my cheeks.

"Why? Why would you ignore this? She bled you dry, dad. Everything you worked so hard for, it's gone. She took all of it, and you let her. You put her name on everything, you gave her the power to ruin you, and she did," I whisper.

With a heavy sigh, he sinks down onto the edge of the bed, resting his elbows on his knees and his head on his hands.

"Do you know how lonely I've been since your mother died?" He asks after a few quiet moments, dropping his hands between his legs to look up at me. "I was a computer nerd. A single father living in a tiny house in the suburbs of New York. Women never looked at me twice, and they certainly wanted nothing to do with me when I couldn't even afford to buy them a drink. Then, suddenly, I had money. I had power and I had status. Allyson came along, beautiful and half my age, and she looked at me twice. She fed my ego and she made me feel good. I'm not stupid, Mackenzie. I know why she was attracted to me, and I know why she agreed to marry me, but I didn't care. I just didn't want to be lonely anymore, and I stupidly thought she would grow to care for me, but it never happened. And then everything snowballed and I didn't know how to stop it. I was in too deep and I didn't want to admit I'd made a mistake. I let you down; I let all of my employees down. I let my need to feel like a man and to stop feeling so lonely ruin everything."

The pain in his voice replaces all of my anger with a sadness so deep I don't know if it will ever go away. I sit down next to him on the bed, grabbing one of his hands and holding it in mine.

"You didn't let me down," I reassure him.

He shakes his head and squeezes my hand.

"Yes, I did. You are the most important person in my life, and I lost sight of that. I should have listened to you. I shouldn't have let you shoulder all of this on your own, and I'm so sorry."

Resting my head on his shoulder, I clasp his hand tighter in mine.

"We'll fix this, dad. I promise, we'll fix this," I tell him quietly.

He yanks his hand out of mine and quickly turns to face me on the end of the bed, pressing his hands to either side of my face and holding it in place.

"No, we won't."

I open my mouth to argue, but he quickly cuts me off.

"This isn't your problem to deal with, Mackenzie. It was never your problem, and you'll never know how sorry I am that I made you feel like it was," he tells me. "I made this mess, and I need to deal with the consequences. On my own. You've shouldered the burden for too long. I let my foolish need to feel wanted and to have someone to take care of again blind me, and I won't let you suffer because of that."

Reaching my hands up, I press them against the top of his that still gently hold onto my face.

"Dad, you still have me. Just because I'm an adult doesn't mean I don't still need my father and need him to take care of me every once in a while."

He laughs, shaking his head at me.

"Honey, you've never needed someone to take care of you. You still won't let me pay off your student loans or buy you a car," he smiles.

"Those student loans are MY debt, not yours. And I live in New York City. No one needs a car in the city," I scoff.

"You're strong and independent, just like you're mother. It's one of the things I love the most about you. I know working for the company wasn't want you wanted, but I was selfish. I was afraid to let you go and spread your wings because I didn't want you to fly away and never come back. So I kept you close and I broke your wings, and I ruined both of us," he says, his voice cracking with emotion.

"You didn't ruin anything. We just got off track for a little while. I'm sorry you were lonely, and I'm sorry that made you jump at someone like Allyson," I whisper.

"I should have listened to you. You didn't like her right from the start, but I figured you'd never approve of anyone who wasn't your mother. I thought it would just take time. But this trip showed me how completely different we are from them. Our families were never meant to be merged and I'm going to rectify that as soon as we get home," he explains.

"You can't just leave her and move on, dad. She has to be punished. She stole *everything* from you. From your company. She put you in hot water with the board and the IRS. We have to make sure she pays for what she's done. I've been going over a plan of action with your accountants. I have meetings scheduled with—"

He cuts me off by pressing one of his fingers against my lips.

"I know. I finally pulled out my laptop this morning when I couldn't sleep and read through all of the emails I've been ignoring. I know how hard you've been working, but it stops now, Mackenzie. No more. I love you, and I adore you for trying to protect me. I'll never be able to forgive myself for sticking my head in the sand all these months. But this isn't your job or your burden to carry anymore."

His words are like a soothing balm to the wounds I've been carrying around inside me all this time. I hate that he's going to have to deal with all of this on his own, but he's right. I can't let it be my problem anymore. I can't put my life on hold for him any longer.

"What am I supposed to do now? Just go back home and pretend like everything is fine?" I ask, suddenly unsure of how exactly I'm supposed to let all of this go, let him go down in flames and just stand back and watch.

"You're supposed to live your own life, be happy, and let me clean up my own messes. I might have turned a blind eye to a lot of things over the last year, but did you think I wouldn't notice the way you've been looking at a certain deckhand who works on this ship?" he asks.

My entire body heats with embarrassment and mortification and he laughs at my expense.

"He seems like a nice, hardworking young man. Obviously no man is good enough for my daughter, and the way he looks at you all the time makes me wish I would have been one of those fathers who threatened a boy with a shotgun when he came sniffing around, but I think he might be just what you need to be happy, and help you live your own life, if you'd let him."

All of the reasons I've been holding back from Declan suddenly melt away. As much as it pains me to let my father handle everything on his own, I have to do what he says. I have to let go, live my own life and find my own happiness.

I know it's crazy, and I know it's a risk, but I don't care. Declan had the guts to open himself up to me and lay his heart on the line, and now it's my turn. I no longer have to worry about distracting him with my problems.

There's nothing holding me back from taking what I want and jumping in with both feet, and that's exactly what I plan on doing.

⚓

"ARE WE THERE yet? Can I take this thing off now?"

"You sound like a toddler. And no, you can't take

the blindfold off yet," Declan laughs as he continues to walk behind me, holding onto my hips and guiding me where I need to go.

I had every intention of spilling my guts to Declan yesterday after I spoke with my father, but he was busy working and I didn't want to bother him by turning myself into that distraction he didn't need. I tried to tell him again last night after everyone went to bed, but *he* distracted *me* by putting on a movie for us in the main salon. Curled up on the couch in front of him under a blanket, with his body pressed up against my back, I stopped paying attention to the movie when his hand slid down into the front of my shorts. After two orgasms and then falling asleep in Declan's arms before the movie ended, I forgot all about talking to him when he woke me up and walked me to my room.

Today, we woke up to find out the captain dropped anchor in the middle of the night due to another round of bad weather he was trying to avoid, and since we were on our way home to St. Thomas, we found ourselves back off the coast of St. John. Allyson and Arianna sent word with one of the stewardesses at breakfast this morning that they both had headaches and wouldn't be coming out of their rooms all day, and my father, now that he had his head back on straight, found himself overwhelmed with emails and phones calls for work. Brooke wanted to do some shopping since we didn't have time when we were here earlier in the trip, and sweet-talked Captain Michael into letting Ben go with her. After they left, Declan found me on the sundeck and told me had a surprise planned for me today.

I've had this damn blindfold on since we got on the jetty and came over to the island, and Declan has refused to let me take it off. I know we got into a vehicle that drove us a few minutes away from the dock, and since we got out he's been steering me in a ton of different directions, but he's remaining tight-lipped about where we're going.

"Can I just have a hint?" I beg.

I feel Declan's lips on the bare skin of my shoulder and he kisses the spot before moving his mouth by my ear.

"Seriously. You're worse than a two-year-old. I take it you don't like surprises."

Just like always, the low rumble of his voice and the feel of his breath against my ear makes me shiver. And having a blindfold over my eyes, being able to hear him and smell him, but not see him, makes me want to ask him to take me back to the ship so we can do other things with the blindfold that require less clothing.

"I love surprises. Especially when I know what they are," I tell him.

I'm immediately rewarded with another laugh from him, and right when I start to tell him about my blindfold idea, he grips onto my hips tighter and forces me to stop walking.

"Okay, you can stop complaining now and take off the blindfold."

Yanking the fabric up from my eyes and over my head, I blink a few times to get used to finally being able to see again and stare out at what I see in front of me in confusion.

"Um, this looks…fun," I state, hoping he doesn't get offended that I have no idea what I'm looking at.

We're standing on a dock, looking at the ocean in front of us, but a large rectangular area of the water, half the size of a football field, has been fenced off. The fencing connects to the dock and there's a small building over to the left, right in the middle of one side of the fence. A man suddenly walks out of the building onto the dock and lifts his hand in a wave to Declan.

"Life jackets are behind you," he shouts to us. "Go on in the water, they'll be out in a few minutes."

Declan waves back, turning away from me and grabbing a life jacket off of an entire rack of them behind us and hands it to me.

"So, we're going swimming in someone's weird, fenced-in ocean pool?" I ask as I shrug into my jacket, clipping the buckles across my chest as Declan does the same with his own life jacket.

"Something like that," he replies with a smile, grabbing my hand and pulling me to the ladder leading down into the water.

After a few minutes of treading water, Declan puts his fingers to his mouth and lets out a loud whistle. I slice my arms through the water and turn my body away from him when I hear a noise come from the building. A gate opens up down below the front of it, and my eyes widen and I let out a gasp when three dolphins come flying out from under the building and zoom through the water towards us.

"We're swimming with dolphins?!" I squeal, unable to keep my excitement contained. "Oh, my God. WE'RE SWIMMING WITH DOLPHINS!"

The three beautiful creatures swim right in between us before circling around and moving away. I can't wipe the smile off of my face as Declan swims up behind me. He wraps one arm around my waist and holds me to him, grabbing my hand and holding it palm down, right underneath the water.

"Your two requests for this trip were to drive a jet ski and swim with dolphins. I couldn't exactly let you accomplish only one of those," he tells me as I watch one of the dolphins break away from the others and head back towards us. "Just keep your hand like this and she'll swim right under it so you can touch her."

I can feel tears stinging my eyes and I blink them away rapidly as the beautiful creature glides through the water right towards me.

"Brooke and I called every dolphin excursion place on every island and they were all booked. How did you do this?" I ask.

"I told you, I have connections working in this business. The owner owed me a favor. Here she comes. Don't be afraid," he tells me softly, pushing my hand deeper under the water.

The dolphin swims right up to us and under my hand, slowing herself down as my palm slides over her sleek, smooth, rubbery skin as she goes.

We spend the next few hours watching the trainer have the dolphins do tricks for us, holding onto their fins and letting them pull us through the water, and ending the best day I've ever had with one of the dolphins coming up out of the water to kiss my cheek.

I watched Declan laugh and enjoy himself even though I'm sure he's done this a bunch of times before, I think about what kind of strings he had to pull to make this day happen for me. I realize right in this moment that I've done it. I've finally gotten a life and it doesn't matter how quickly it happened or that it started off as a fling. This is what I want. This is what makes me happy—being with this man who drives me crazy as much as he makes me smile, and I don't care what kind of obstacles stand in our way, I want more of this life. I want it all.

I just have to tell that to Declan and hope he still meant what he said when he told me I made him want to change his course.

CHAPTER 23

⚓

Declan

I HAVEN'T BEEN able to wipe the sappy grin off my face for the last two days, ever since I surprised Mackenzie with the dolphin swim. Even knowing tonight is the last night Mackenzie and her family will be on the ship isn't going to bring me down, because I have a plan and I'm sticking to it.

After my morning meeting with Ben and Eddie yesterday, going over everyone's duties, the three of us walked around doing preventative maintenance on the ship. When I was finishing things up on the sundeck, Mackenzie came running up to me with a nervous smile on her face and an anxious bounce to her step. When she told me she had something important to talk to me about as soon as I could get away from work, I told her not to worry about anything and I had something to show her first. I knew the things I'd said to her that night in the wheelhouse scared her, but I didn't want her worrying about any of that. I just wanted her to be happy, have fun, and learn a little more about me.

Grabbing her hand, I took her with me as I finished up my chores around the ship. Then, I took her on a much more in-depth tour from what she got when she first boarded. That initial tour only included a quick safety lesson and all the amenities in the guest quarters. I took her to the engine room and introduced her to the guys down there and I showed her all of the inner workings of the machinery. We walked around every inch of the ship and I explained to her what everything is used for. We sat down on the deck and I taught her all the different knots we use, completely amazed at how quickly she picked them up, tying a Figure 8 Knot faster than even Ben can.

We laughed, we talked, we had fun, and most importantly, I showed her all the reasons why I love being on a boat so much, hoping she'd understand and feel the same. At the end of the day, as we watched the sun set off in the horizon and she helped me fold up all the deck chairs, she made a comment about how she might like to work on a boat, getting away from everything and traveling the world.

And that's why I haven't been able to wipe the damn smile off my face since then.

"Hey there, handsome."

My body jerks away from the palms running up my

back, and the mop in my hand that I was using to wipe off the deck around the Jacuzzi drops from my hands and clatters to the floor when I turn around.

"Good morning, Mrs. Armstrong. Is there something you need?" I ask in the politest voice I can muster, smiling at Allyson who's standing in front of me in the skimpiest bathing suit I've ever seen. I want to take a shower in bleach from having her hands on me.

She takes a step towards me, pressing her fake tits up against my chest and running one claw-like fingernail down the side of my cheek. I've had a lot of female guests hit on me over the years, and it's always a struggle to remain professional and nice without bruising their ego by telling them they're the last woman on earth you'd ever get mixed up with.

Aside from the fact she's the biggest bitch I've ever come in contact with, she's so disgustingly skinny that her ribs and the sharp bones of her hips stick out. All I can think about as she stands here, staring up at me with a seductive smile on her face and her rock hard, too-big-for-her-body tits smashed against my chest, are the soft curves on Mackenzie, her full and all natural breasts that feel perfect in my hands, and the gorgeous smile that lights up her entire face.

"It's Mrs. *Drake-Swanson*-Armstrong," she corrects me, her hand flattening against my chest and slowly moving down over my abs. "And there's definitely something you can help me with."

I grab her wrist and pull it away from me right when her hand gets to the waistband of my shorts. I have no idea what kind of shit this woman is trying to pull, but I don't have time for it right now, and all she's doing is making a fool of herself.

"Ma'am, I think you should probably go find your husband and let me get back to work. How about I radio down to the chef, have him set up a nice, romantic lunch just for the two of you?" I suggest with a smile, dropping her hand and moving back to bend down and pick up the mop, holding it in front of me and using it as a shield.

"Things between Mr. Armstrong and I aren't going very well," she says with a wave of her hand. "I heard a rumor that you're about to become a captain. That sounds *very* exciting. I think the two of us should go find a quiet place to relax and you can tell me all about your boat and where you plan on taking me on it."

I want to laugh right in her face. Does this shit really work on other men? Obviously it must, considering she landed Mackenzie's dad. Seeing the look of complete confidence on her face as she struts closer to me again proves she thinks it will work this time as well.

Holding my hand up to stop her, she pauses, putting her hands on her hips and thrusting her chest out, like the power of her tits is going to make me drop to my knees and agree to whatever this shit is she's offering.

"I'm flattered, Mrs. *Drake-Swanson-Armstrong*," I tell

her, stressing the string of names she made a point to correct me on, swallowing back the bile that rises in my throat. "I don't know what exactly you heard, but I don't own a boat. I can barely afford a canoe, let alone a multi-million-dollar yacht."

I laugh good-naturedly, expecting her to laugh right along with me at her mistake and make up some sort of excuse about how she was just teasing me, but she doesn't. Her seductive smile turns into a lip-curling sneer of disgust and she crosses her arms across her chest.

"Don't be flattered, I was just taking pity on you and trying to make you feel better after what my stepdaughter has done to you," she scoffs with a roll of her eyes.

At the mention of Mackenzie, all the politeness and professionalism I'd been holding onto vanishes in the blink of an eye.

"What the hell are you talking about?"

She laughs, shaking her head at me.

"You poor, gullible man. Do you have any idea how many vacation flings that girl has had, and how many men, just like you, she's left in her wake? It's pathetic, really. The way they fall all over her and fall for her lies."

I refuse to let myself believe her words. She's a bitch, and even an idiot could see that she and Mackenzie don't get along. There's no way Mackenzie did this before. There's no way she'd lie to me about something like that.

You've known her less than two weeks. Do you really think you know her all that well?

I ignore my conscience and the rapid beat of my heart as Allyson keeps going, sticking the knife in a little deeper.

"I bet she told you she'd never had a vacation fling before. Started off by telling you she wanted to do something fun to take her mind off of all her little problems, how she wasn't looking for a white picket fence or for you to throw away all your hopes and dreams over someone you just met," she says, clasping her hands together by her heart and talking in a dreamy voice like she's reading a fairytale in a children's book.

I'd be annoyed and disgusted with Allyson's behavior if the things she's saying weren't the EXACT same things Mackenzie had said to me the day I took her out on the jet ski to the coral reef. I want to tell Allyson to shut the fuck up, but I can't move, I can't think, and I can't fucking speak as she takes the knife she's lodged in my chest and turns it.

"And then things changed," Allyson continues, dropping her hands to her sides. "She stuck her claws in deep, made you want more, and made you think *she* wanted more. She showed interest in those hopes and dreams of yours and made you think she wanted to be a part of them."

Allyson throws her head back and laughs while I

continue standing in front of her, holding onto the wooden handle of the mop so tightly that it's seconds away from snapping in half.

"I've been telling my husband for months he needs to get a handle on that girl, but he doesn't listen. He just lets her run wild, breaking hearts all over the place, and it looks like she just did it again going by the look on your face."

She makes a *tsk'ing* sound with her tongue, shaking her head at me.

"But honestly, do you have any idea how much her father is worth? Did you really think you had a shot?"

Allyson studies me for a few quiet seconds while I clench my teeth so hard that I wait for one of them to crack.

"Oh, my God. You did!" she laughs again. "You actually thought you had a shot with Mark Armstrong's little princess. The one who will inherit EVERYTHING he owns. The one who can get anything her little heart desires with just the snap of her fingers. She's got men lined up back in New York just waiting for her to come home and finally pick one and put them out of their misery. Men her father handpicked, with pedigrees, college educations, and money in the bank. They can give her things like security and stability. What exactly can you give her, other than life on a stupid little boat, that you don't even *own*?"

I can physically feel my heart cracking in half, sending a shooting pain through my chest that robs the breath from my lungs and makes my knees want to give out, but I hold my head up high and push everything back, refusing to let this woman see that her words have hit their desired target.

"I'm sorry you fell for that little innocent, 'I'm just a regular girl' act of hers. When you're ready for a *real* woman, you know where to find me."

With that, Allyson turns and waltzes away, taking my fucking broken heart with her as she goes.

I'M A PUSSY and a fucking coward. Instead of confronting Mackenzie as soon as Allyson walked away from me earlier, I spent the day avoiding her and letting everything her stepmother said stew and fester until I was analyzing every word Mackenzie had ever said to me and every minute we'd spent together. She seemed so honest, so sweet and so *real*, but now I can't stop thinking that it was all an act. I can't stop wondering if everything Allyson said was the truth and everything Mackenzie said was a lie. I want to trust Mackenzie and trust what I feel for her, but I can't stop reminding myself that I barely know her. I've spent less than two weeks with her. Now that the idea has been planted, all I can think about are those men waiting for her back home. Men who are better than me, men with more money than me, men who can give her the security and stability I'll never be able to, and it's eating me up inside.

I knew she was holding something back, and like an idiot, I let it go and gave her time to come to me, to open herself up and give me everything. I realize now what she was holding back was probably the fact that she had better offers back in New York. Ones her father would approve of. Maybe she really did feel something for me, and I didn't imagine the way she looked at me and the way she believed in me. Maybe she really thought we could have a future, but I was kidding myself for thinking I could be the one to give it to her.

As tied up in knots as I am over all of this, I still can't stop wanting her. I still can't stop needing her. I still can't stop wishing I had enough to give her and hoping that everything Allyson said to me was all a bunch of bullshit meant to scare me away.

I'm a pussy, and I'm a fucking coward, because it did the trick.

"There you are. I've been looking everywhere for you."

I close my eyes for a few minutes, wishing my heart didn't still beat in double-time when I hear Mackenzie's voice. Wishing I was immune to her and could just walk away without another look back.

Setting the tray of glasses from lunch on the counter in the stew pantry, I take a deep breath and turn around to find Mackenzie leaning against the counter in the galley, smiling at me with that soft, gorgeous smile of hers that lights up her entire face. I mentally yank the knife out of my chest Allyson stuck in there earlier, giving Mackenzie a smirk instead of wincing in pain.

"Well, you found me. What can I help you with?"

She rounds the edge of the island and walks over to the door of the pantry to stand in front of me.

"I just wanted to see what time you got off work. Thought we could do something fun tonight and talk before tomorrow gets here. I've got a problem I need your help with."

Tomorrow. Her last morning on the boat and the day she'll walk out of my life and back to all the offers and opportunities waiting for her back home with the snap of her fingers.

"Right, tomorrow will be here before you know it," I reply with a light, breezy attitude I'm definitely not feeling. "I'm guessing you're referring to the problem with your job? I'm sure you have nothing to worry about. It's not like you need to work anyway, right?"

I laugh at my attempt at a joke, wanting to throw up with each fucking painful chuckle that comes out of my mouth.

Nothing about this is funny. Not the words that I'm saying and not the way Mackenzie's smile immediately drops and all the blood rushes from her face. I want to take back the words I just said, but what's the point? They're true. Even if everything between us wasn't a lie, even if every word out of Allyson's mouth was bullshit, a lot of it was still right on target. Mackenzie has a perfect life waiting for her back in New York. And even if she pays her own way and doesn't take a penny of her father's money, she still *can*. And that's the problem. I will never be able to give her that kind of safety or stability.

"But you're right," I continue with a fake fucking smile, ignoring the look of pain written all over her face, telling myself it doesn't matter and she'll be fine. "We should do something fun to celebrate your last day stuck on this boring, stupid boat. I get off work at nine. Meet me up on the sundeck and we'll have a late dinner."

I know I shouldn't make these plans with her. I know I should just leave her alone and let her walk away, but I'm a Goddamn glutton for punishment. As much as I know it will hurt, I need this last night with her. I need one more night of being close to her. One more night of pretending like something more between us could actually work before I rip the Band-Aid off and come crashing back down to reality.

Bending down, I kiss the top of her head, clenching my hands into fists so I don't wrap my arms around her, beg for her forgiveness and tell her I didn't mean anything I said. I walk around her, whistling as I go, jamming my fists into the pockets of my shorts before I punch the wall of the galley on my way out.

I'm a pussy, and a fucking coward.

CHAPTER 24

⚓

Mackenzie

A LLYSON AND ARIANNA supposedly started coming down with some sort of flu on our final leg of the journey back to St. Thomas, and I can't say I'm not incredibly happy the over-the-top, formal dinner for our last night on the ship was cancelled. I was in no mood to wear a fancy dress, do my hair or put on make-up, and sit around a table pretending like I didn't want to pick up my knife and stab both of them for what they'd done to my father.

Something tells me they don't really have the flu, and they're staying locked away together in Arianna's room because my father told Allyson immediately after we talked, in no uncertain terms, that her life was over. That he knew what she'd been doing, and he'd be handing it all over to the authorities once we got back to St. Thomas, as well as handing her divorce papers.

I wanted to cheer and shout and be happy that my father finally stood up for himself and took back control of his life, and couldn't wait to find Declan and tell him everything.

That excitement was short-lived when I found him down in the galley earlier. I was now in no mood to do anything other than curl up in a ball in my room and cry until I had nothing left in me. I planned on doing exactly that for the rest of the night, especially when Brooke found me and told me dinner was cancelled.

Of course I couldn't hide what happened or pretend like everything was fine when my face was red and splotchy and my eyes were puffy from crying for hours. I told her everything that happened with my father. I told her it made me realize it was time to get a life and that I wanted that life to begin and end with Declan. I told her I was falling in love with him, and he just shattered my heart into a thousand pieces with his callous words.

She cursed his name and got angry on my behalf, but all I could do was stay curled up in a ball in the bed, unable to make my limbs move an inch.

Had I been wrong about him all this time? Had I misjudged or misheard the things he said to me in the wheelhouse that night? How could I be so stupid? How could I think that a man I just met would ask me to stay with him and never leave?

"That's it. Get your ass out of bed and get in the

shower," Brooke suddenly orders, sliding out of bed from behind me where she'd been holding me and letting me cry into my pillow.

"I don't want to," I sniffle.

"I know you don't. I know you're pissed and you're hurt and you're sad, but this is your last night on this boat. Your last night with Declan."

She comes around to my side of the bed and I glare up at her when she says his name.

"I know. He's an asshole and I really want to go find him and chop off his balls, but you need to do this for *you*, not for him. If you skip out on this dinner with him, avoid him, and walk off this boat tomorrow without looking back, you're going to regret it. Take a shower, get dressed, hold your head up high and show him what he's missing. Show him just how royally he fucked up," Brooke demands.

I close my eyes and burrow my face into my pillow, wishing she wasn't right. Spending the evening with him will kill me, but I know it would hurt even worse if I walk away tomorrow without even trying, always wondering "what if."

With a sigh, I pull myself out of bed and head for the shower.

WEARING MY FAVORITE pair of jean shorts and a fitted t-shirt I got from St. Thomas before we boarded the ship almost two weeks ago, I make my way along the outside deck, running my hand along the railing as I go, staring out at the dark water we're slowly making our way through while the gentle ocean breeze rustles my hair around my face.

My bare feet come to a stuttering stop when I get around to the sundeck and see what Declan has done.

The lounge chairs have all been folded up and put away, and he's spread a blanket out on the floor in the middle of the deck. The blanket has been set up just like the table usually is for dinner—with two white plates and silver domes covering them, silverware and crystal glasses, napkins folded into elegant shapes, and a large vase in the middle filled with fresh flowers. Dotting the blanket, and set up all around it, are small glass candleholders with flickering tea light candles lit inside.

"You're beautiful."

Declan's voice brings my head up from the spread in front of me. I find him leaning his shoulder against the side of the ship with his hands in the front pockets of his cargo shorts, staring at me. His eyes heat my skin as they slowly travel up my bare legs and across my torso to my face. The corner of his mouth tips up into a smile and I press one hand to my stomach, the sight of his dimples making me want to jump over the blanket to kiss him and cry at the same time.

After tomorrow morning, I'll never see those dimples again. I'll never hear his voice telling me I'm

TARA SIVEC

beautiful and actually making me believe it. He went along with me keeping things light and easy, and we've had fun together the last few days, but then he went and ruined it all and made me second-guess everything we'd shared. Now that the moment is here, now that it's almost time for me to leave him, I wish I'd told him everything I wanted to say. I wish I had the courage to do it now, in spite of how wrong I was about him. I hate myself for being a coward. I hate myself for not wanting to ruin our last night together, even though he ruined what I thought I could have for my future.

"I'm wearing ratty jean shorts and a t-shirt," I tell him with a raise of one eyebrow, breaking his stare to look down at myself and joke about the "beautiful" comment, even though it's taking everything in me to remain calm and casual when all I want to do is break down and cry again.

"You could be wearing a potato sack and you'd still be the most beautiful woman I've ever seen," he replies softly, pushing away from the wall to walk over to the opposite side of the blanket from me.

He gestures with his hand for me to join him, and I paste a smile on my face, taking the few remaining steps to the edge of the blanket.

We both sit down across from each other, and he reaches towards me, wrapping his hand around the handle of the silver dome on top of my plate, as well as the one in front of him.

"I asked Marcel to make something fancy and special for tonight."

With a flourish, he whips both domes off at the same time, and I can't help but laugh loudly when I see what he's had Marcel make.

"Cheeseburgers and french fries!" I exclaim, clasping my hands together and holding them against my heart. "My favorite."

"Only the best for my girl."

My hands slowly drop down into my lap and I keep the smile on my face, even though my eyes burn with tears. I don't know why he called me that, and I hate how it makes my heart flutter when I know it's not true.

I just want him to take back what he said to me in the galley. I want him to apologize, tell me he was wrong and I was right. Tell me I wasn't imagining things in the wheelhouse the other night and that I still make him want to break all the rules and change his plans.

I just want him to ask me to stay.

We eat our dinner in silence, listening to the waves crash against the side of the ship that brings me closer and closer to the moment I'll have to leave him. It takes a lot of effort for me to eat, swallowing past the huge lump in my throat, but I finish everything, not wanting him to think I don't like or appreciate the meal he had Marcel prepare for us. Wanting him to think I'm perfectly fine this thing between us isn't going any further and that I'll be perfectly fine when I get off that ship tomorrow and never see him again.

Declan quietly clears off the blanket, moving everything to a tray on the table a few feet away, before joining me again. He lies down on his back next to me, grabbing my elbow and tugging me down. I curl up into his side with my head in the crook of his arm that's resting on the blanket behind my back, and we stare up at the stars in the clear sky above us.

"What was your favorite part of your vacation?" he asks softly.

I turn my head to find him looking down at me instead of the stars.

You. My favorite part of this vacation was you. Every minute I spent with you, until you realized you'd made a mistake and pushed me away.

"That's a tough one. Probably driving a jet ski for the first time and doing my best to chuck you off the back of it," I joke, knowing if I say anything else, I'll burst into tears.

He laughs, his smile growing wider as he twirls a lock of my hair in his fingers, looking away from me and back up to the sky.

"What's your favorite part of your job?" I ask, unable to take my eyes away from his profile, studying it and memorizing it so I'll never forget it.

"Everything. But I guess the travel. Getting to see new places and always waking up somewhere new. I'm not very good at staying in one place for very long. I get grumpy and anxious to move around. I know you don't like your job very much, but at least it pays well. At least it's secure and stable. I don't even have two fucking nickels to rub together, but that's just the way I like it."

I blink back the tears as he continues to watch the stars, hearing the irritation in his voice and not believing a word he says. I don't know why he's saying these things to me and it makes me want to push myself away from him, scream at him that I no longer have a well-paying job or a job of any kind. That my life is anything but secure and stable right now and that I wanted more than anything for him to give that to me. I don't care if he has all the money in the world or not a cent to his name. I just wanted *him*, and I don't understand why he couldn't see that. I don't understand why it matters.

Keeping my thoughts to myself, I know without a doubt that I'm doing the right thing by not laying my heart out and telling him everything. What the hell kind of future could we even have? I live in New York and he lives on a boat.

I just want him to ask me to stay.

"You're absolutely right. My life is perfect back in New York. I was just having a moment. You're going to make a great captain," I tell him, hiding my lies behind reassurance that I believe in him and I'm happy for what his future holds, even if he doesn't want me in it.

"Mackenzie," he whispers, his face turning back to mine.

I don't know what he's about to say, and I don't want to know. If he tells me something flippant, like he had fun and he'll miss having me around to keep him on his toes just to keep things light and easy, it will belittle everything I'm feeling right now and ruin this moment.

Instead of letting him finish, letting him hurt my feelings and break my heart even more, I press my hand against his mouth, wanting something good to remember about this moment instead of something that will destroy me.

"Not right now. I don't want to think about anything else right now," I tell him.

Declan turns on his side to face me, his arm around my shoulder moving down around my back to tug me closer to his body. He wraps his free hand around my wrist, pulling my hand away from his mouth to press my palm against his heart, trapping it between us.

Without saying a word, he gives me what I want and makes me stop thinking about anything else but the two of us and this perfect moment, lying under the stars on the deck of a yacht.

He moves his head closer and I close my eyes when he presses his lips to mine. The kiss is slow, and soft and sweet, and I pour everything into it as I swipe my tongue through his mouth, letting him know without words how I really feel. How I wish I had the courage to tell him. He keeps my hand pressed to his chest and deepens the kiss, sliding his arm down my back until he's clutching my ass and pulling my lower body flush against his.

I can't deny my body's reaction to him, even after the words he said to me today. I can't stop wanting him, needing him, and craving him. My hips rock against his, feeling how hard he is for me. I let go and let myself be okay with the fact that at least we still have this, and neither one of us can hide it behind silence and fear, or shitty words and pretending.

Declan suddenly pulls his mouth away from mine, his eyes dark and his heart thumping rapidly under the palm of my hand as he looks down at me.

"Come back to my room with me."

It's not a question and it's not a demand. His voice is soft and low and there's an edge to it that tells me this is a plea. He's begging me, and there's nothing I can do but say yes.

I nod in response and he helps me up from the blanket, grabbing my hand and pulling me through the sliding glass doors into the ship, leaving everything behind in our haste to get to his bunk.

We quietly move through the dark ship, a few softly glowing nightlights guiding our way across the formal dining room, downstairs through the galley, and into his room. It's in the same small hallway where the laundry room is located, right across the hall from it, and I can't ignore the sting of tears when I remember the first night we were together, and how easy and uncomplicated it was.

As Declan quietly turns the handle to his room and pulls me inside, I know everything that happens after this moment will confuse my already muddied heart and mind, but I can't deny him what he wants. I can't deny myself what *I* want, and I want him, however I can have him, one last time.

We squeeze together on the tiny bottom bunk in his room, neither of us saying a word as we slowly undress each other, easily laughing when Declan hits his head on the bottom of the top bunk and when I slam my elbow against the wall trying to remove his shirt.

He rolls on top of me and I wrap my legs around his hips and my arms around his shoulders. His hands slide under my back and he pulls my body as close to his as possible, kissing me softly as he enters me slowly. Our arms stay locked around each other as we move together, neither of us in a hurry for this to end.

There are no dirty words whispered in my ear this time, no quick and frenzied fucking, just slow and steady and more powerful than anything I've felt before.

I press my hands to either side of his face as my hips move against him, taking him deeper and loving the way he moans my name. His forehead rests against mine and I close my eyes as he rocks his body into me, the slow push and pull of his cock in and out of me lighting my body on fire and making me ramble in French. It's easy to say the words, to tell him everything

I wish I had the guts to say, when he has no idea what they mean.

"Demande-moi de rester. Je ne veux jamais te quitter. S'il te plait, demande-moi de rester," I whisper with my eyes still tightly closed and our foreheads pressed together.

My softly spoken words do exactly what I expected them to. Declan groans my name and starts moving his hips faster, taking me harder, slamming into me rougher. It doesn't matter that I want this to last forever, it's impossible to slow down my release when he's so deep inside me, swiveling his hips in a slow circle and hitting just the right spot over and over, holding me tight. His eyes never leave mine as my orgasm works its way up my body and explodes out of me. I tighten my legs around him and bury my face in the side of his neck as I come, my voice muffled as I whisper his name.

Declan's hands slide down to my ass and he tips my hips up, pumping into me faster as he follows right behind me, quickly finding his own release with my name on his lips before collapsing on top of me.

I lose track of time as we stay locked together. Our arms are still around each other, and Declan is still inside of me. I know I will never feel as safe and secure and *whole* as I do right now, with the heavy weight of his body on top of mine, and I keep my face pressed against the side of his neck so he won't see my tears.

He can deny it all he wants, make flippant comments, and pretend like light and easy is all he wants from me now, and make me second-guess everything that happened between us, but I know he's lying. I know he feels something more for me, and I know he wants me to change his plans, even if he won't say the words again. I have no idea what happened to make him act like this, and I'm too much of a coward to question him.

I just want him to ask me to stay, but he never does.

CHAPTER 25

Declan

WATCHING MACKENZIE AND her family say good-bye to the crew, letting her walk off the ship without saying anything was the hardest fucking thing I've ever done. Standing in a line next to the rest of the crew, I had to remain stoic and professional when Mackenzie, her father, and Brooke walked down the line, shaking each of our hands and thanking us for a wonderful trip, when all I wanted to do was pull her away from everyone and tell her I fucked up. Tell her I didn't care about not being good enough for her because I'd spend the rest of my life making sure I got there and gave her everything she deserved.

Allyson and Arianna were absent from the good-bye, and according to Zoe, they got off before everyone else woke up, probably because they didn't give a shit about pleasantries and thank you's. I didn't care where they were, I didn't care about anything but the fact that I let the best thing that's ever happened to me just fucking walk away.

I almost dropped to my knees when her small hand slid into mine. I almost cried like a fucking baby when she looked up at me with a sad smile on her face and told me it was fun, but it was time for her to get back to the good life she left behind.

The good fucking life that I wouldn't be a part of and it was my own damn fault. I knew she didn't care about money. I knew she didn't care about whatever guys were waiting for her back home, ready to give her whatever she wanted. I knew she wasn't the type of woman who gave a shit about what someone had as long as they were a decent human being and treated her with respect.

I treated her like shit. I took everything I knew about her, let her bitch of a stepmother poison me with lies and make me believe things that weren't true, and I hurt her in the worst way possible. She'd opened up to me and told me she was miserable working for her father, and I threw it right back in her face, made a joke out of it, and made a demeaning comment about how she didn't really need to work.

I stopped trying to convince her to stay, and pushed her away instead.

For the last two days, ever since I watched her walk off this ship, I've spent my time in the bottom of a bottle when I'm not working to get ready for the next charter. I've tried drinking away all the shitty things I said to her, wishing it would erase them from my mind and make them not true, but it hasn't worked. Nothing works. Nothing will erase what I did to her, nothing will erase the smell of her from my pillows and my sheets from our last night together, nothing will erase her smile, or her laugh, or her touch, or the sound of my name on her lips.

I let her slip right out of my hands, and I have no one to blame but myself.

"You look like shit," Zoe announces, walking into the crew mess and flopping down on the bench seat next to me, Ben following behind her and taking a seat on the other side of me.

He leans over and sniffs my shoulder.

"Jesus, you smell like shit too," he complains, pulling back and giving me a disgusted look.

I bring the half-empty bottle of whiskey up to my mouth, but Zoe snatches it away and slams it down on the table.

"That's enough. You're cut off."

Glaring at her, I reach for the bottle but she smacks my hand away.

"Nope. No more," she informs me, sliding the bottle further out of my reach. "We've let you sit here feeling sorry for yourself for two days, and it ends now."

Resting my elbows on the table, I put my head in my hands and close my eyes.

"I fucked up," I mutter.

"We know," Ben and Zoe reply in unison.

"I don't know how to fix it."

Ben sighs and I drop my hands to the table to look at him.

"I can't believe you didn't ask her to stay, man. I thought that's where your mind was at. I thought that's what you wanted. Then, the next thing I know, she's walking off the ship looking like you just kicked her puppy and Brooke is telling me if you're anywhere around when she comes to see me next month she'll cut your dick off," Ben says.

"Why in the hell would I ever ask her to stay? To do what, hang around on the ship and watch me work? She has a life and a job and it's all back in New York. I don't fit in her world and she doesn't fit in mine," I tell him, knowing I'm lying. Even if I don't fit into her world, she absolutely fits into mine.

And knowing that right now, I miss her so much and I hurt so much inside without her here that I don't give a shit who doesn't fit where. I'll do whatever it takes to *make* everything fit.

"I know you don't believe that shit, so why are you saying it? Who are you trying to convince? Because I damn sure know it's not true," Ben argues. "I've never seen you so fucking happy. I've never seen you want something more than what this ship has to offer. I'm not saying it's not an awesome thing that you have a goal and a dream. I'm just saying, it's good to have more than one. It's good to have something else to come home to when you have a shitty day. She could have been your home, and you fucked it all up because you're so hung up on the fact that she has money and you don't."

I *thought* I was hung up on that. Allyson made me believe I couldn't give her what she wanted and I wasn't good enough for her, but I can't lie to myself anymore. I might not be able to buy her things, but I can give her something worth a whole hell of a lot more. I can give her my heart and my soul and my promise to do whatever it takes to make her never feel like anything is lacking from her life. I can give her every piece of me and beg her to never let go.

"I'm not hung up on that shit. I was. I mean, I got confused for a little bit, but I know it's not important. I know she doesn't care about those things and none of that matters," I tell Ben quietly.

"Thank fucking God," Zoe mutters. "I really didn't want to have to beat the shit out of you to get you to see the light."

I smile at her, but I don't have the energy to laugh. My chest is too tight wondering what the hell I'm going to do to get Mackenzie back, and my stomach is starting to churn with all the alcohol I consumed in the last two days.

"How the hell am I going to fix this? I know I was an asshole, but she agreed with me. She told me her life is perfect back in New York. She told me she was just having a moment when she said she hated her job and didn't know what to do with her life. Am I really supposed to chase after her, ask her to leave her perfect life where she can have anything she wants, and tell her to take a chance, living on a fucking boat with me?" I ask, rambling like an idiot as my heart starts beating faster with nerves.

"Yes, you dumb shit. And she lied."

All three of us look up at Marcel when he walks into the room, tossing a printout of a *New York Times* article onto the table in front of us.

"What the hell are you talking about?"

"Since when do you speak English?" Zoe asks in shock.

He ignores her, pressing his palms on top of the table and leaning over it towards me.

"You make a stupid comment about how at least she doesn't need to worry about going back home, because it's not like she needs to really work anyway, and you're surprised she didn't tell you the truth? You lied, so she lied. Stop being a dumb shit and get your head out of your ass," Marcel scolds, smacking his hand against the newspaper article and sliding it closer to me.

"Dude, you told her it's not like she needs to work

anyway? Ouch. No wonder you've been bathing in whiskey and Brooke wants to cut off your balls," Ben mutters.

"Oh, my God," I whisper, all of that whiskey Ben mentioned bubbling in my stomach and threatening to come right back up all over the table when I see the headline for the front page story in the *Times* and the corresponding article.

"Mark Armstrong, multi-millionaire and owner of Armstrong Industries, the industry leader in software applications, filed for bankruptcy yesterday morning after the culmination of a six-month long investigation," Zoe reads over my shoulder. "The investigation, led by his daughter, Mackenzie Armstrong, resulted in indisputable proof that Mr. Armstrong's wife of one year, Allyson Drake-Swanson-Armstrong, has been funneling money from Armstrong Industries, as well as Mr. Armstrong's personal accounts, into offshore foreign accounts, for the entirety of their marriage. Charges are being brought against Mrs. Drake-Swanson-Armstrong and she is currently being held at Albion Correctional Facility in Albion, New York until trial. Mrs. Drake-Swanson-Armstrong's daughter, Arianna, has entered into a plea bargain, swearing she had no knowledge of her mother's deeds, and is hoping to have all charges against her dropped. The prosecution is still trying to uncover where all of Mr. Armstrong's money disappeared, but it looks like Armstrong Industries will be closing its doors for good after this weekend, letting go of over three-hundred and seventy-five employees, including Mr. Armstrong's daughter. Mr. Armstrong and his daughter are currently out of the country, and unavailable to comment on the possibility that Mr. Armstrong will also find himself doing jail time, due to his inability to pay his business and personal federal taxes."

All of us are silent in the small dining area when Zoe finishes reading the article. My head spins and I feel like I can't breathe.

"He doesn't have a lot of time for me, and he's been ignoring problems that have been staring him in the face for months. I'm not really looking forward to going back home, where reality is going to crash like a bull in a China shop, and he won't be able to ignore things anymore. At work or at home."

Mackenzie's words from the night we had dinner at Rhythms on St. Croix come crashing back into my head. She told me…I just didn't listen. I never imagined she had something so huge resting on her shoulders. Something that would make her hesitant to make promises to me or scared to take hold of something she wanted when her father's life was falling apart. Of course she lied and told me her life was perfect. Why in the hell would she be honest with me when I didn't take her problems seriously?

"There are things going on in my life back home. Things I can't—"

I hear her voice in my head the night in the wheelhouse. The night I told her she made me want to change all of my plans. I could see the fear and uneasiness in her eyes, and I thought it was because she just wasn't sure about *me*. Wasn't sure about *us*. She was trying to tell me and I cut her off. Then I stopped her from talking to me AGAIN a few days later and took her on a tour of the ship instead. I didn't listen, and I didn't give her a chance to explain because I was too afraid she'd list all the reasons why this couldn't work between us. I was selfish, and I let Allyson bring forward all of those insecurities until I pushed her away.

She needed me and I fucking pushed her away.

"Marcel, Mackenzie said something to me in French the other night. Demande-moi de rester. Je ne veux jamais te quitter. S'il te plait, demande-moi de rester," I tell him, repeating her words that have been playing on a loop in my head ever since she said them. "What did she say?"

Her voice was so quiet and sad, but I just assumed she said something to turn me on, because she knew what the sound of her speaking in French did to me. But I couldn't stop thinking about the *way* she said those words. It was different. It meant something more; I can feel it in my gut.

"You dumb shit," Marcel curses, shaking his head and glaring at me.

My hands start to shake, and I know. I *know* what

he's going to say next will break me in half, but I need to hear it. I need to know what she whispered. What she wanted me to hear, but at the same time, didn't want to say.

"What did she say, dammit?!" I shout, slamming my fist on the table, making Zoe jump next to me at my outburst.

Marcel rolls his eyes at me, but gives me what I want.

"She said, *'Ask me to stay. I never want to leave you. Please, ask me to stay.'* You dumb shit."

Everything in the room fades away until all I can hear is the rushing of blood and the pounding of my own heart in my ears. Ben is muttering under his breath, Zoe is calling me an idiot, and Marcel is back to cursing at me in French, but I don't hear any of it. All I can hear is Mackenzie's voice, begging me to ask her to stay.

"Goddammit. GOD FUCKING DAMMIT!" I shout, crumbling up the printed article and throwing it across the room, sliding down the bench seat to get the hell out from behind this table.

"Move. FUCKING MOVE!" I yell at Ben when he doesn't get out of my way fast enough.

He scrambles out from behind the table and backs up against the wall, holding his hands in the air to give me room. I take off running down the hall, ignoring Jessica, Ashley, and Eddie when they open their bunk doors and ask what's going on as I race past.

Ben, Zoe, and Marcel all follow after me as I fly up the stairs, through the guest quarters and out onto the deck, running as fast as I can to the bridge still hooked up to the dock.

"Declan, where the hell are you going?" Ben shouts after me as my feet pound across the wooden planks.

"I'm going to find Mackenzie!" I yell back to him, jumping onto the dock. "I'm going to apologize, and then I'm going to fucking beg her to stay."

I hear everyone let out a cheer back on the deck of the boat, but I ignore it and keep on running. I never should have let her go, and there's no way in hell I'm letting her leave this island without telling her.

CHAPTER 26

⚓

Mackenzie

"I S EVERYTHING OKAY, Mackenzie?"

My head comes up from staring at my plate where I'd been pushing my food around to give my dad a smile.

"It's fine. I'm fine," I reassure him, even though nothing is fine and I don't know if it ever will be again.

He knows I'm lying, but he doesn't argue with me, thank God. I've cried enough tears in the last two days that if he says anything about the man who made me shed them, I won't be able to stop myself from breaking down again. The only bright spot in getting off the ship was not having Allyson and Arianna there with us. They left before the rest of us woke up, and by the time my father, Brooke, and I made it back to the hotel where we were staying until our flight home tomorrow morning, the local authorities already had them in handcuffs and were escorting them out of the hotel and into awaiting police cars.

The only time I smiled in the last two days was when Allyson saw us standing there watching them being taken away, and she turned on the waterworks, crying and apologizing and begging for us to help her. Hearing my father tell her to "Fuck off and go to hell" was one of the best moments of my life, and I couldn't have been more proud of him.

But once that excitement wore off, once they were driven away and out of our lives, reality sunk in. The reality that my father might have gotten rid of one problem, but he still had a thousand more to deal with once we got back to New York. And the reality that even though we'd mended our relationship and were closer than ever, I felt more alone than I'd ever been.

I hated that I wanted nothing more than to pick up the phone and call Declan back on the ship and tell him what happened. I cried myself to sleep the last two nights feeling so cold and lonely in my bed, wishing he was there with me, holding me in his arms and telling me everything would be okay.

Nothing would ever be okay again. Even if my father managed to get himself out of all the trouble that awaited him in New York, I knew *I'd* never be okay again. I left my heart back on the *Helios*, and it was impossible to get it back. Part of me couldn't wait to get on the plane tomorrow so I could put as much distance between myself and what happened on that ship, but I knew, no matter how far away I went, I'd never be able to forget. I'd never be able to close my eyes and not hear his voice, not feel his hands on me, not see the happiness on his face when he talked about becoming a captain, and never stop wondering what would have happened if he'd just asked me to stay.

I just wanted him to ask me to stay.

I had been right all along. I wasn't the type of woman who could have a vacation fling and walk away unscathed. I fell in love with the strong, gorgeous, stubborn man who behaved like an asshole more times than I can count. I fell in love with his passion for his job, and I fell in love with his confidence, and I even fell in love with how quickly he could realize he did something wrong and apologize. I fell in love with the fantasy of spending the rest of my days traveling the world with him and the excitement of falling in love with all of the things I hadn't learned about him yet.

I fell in love with a man I met on vacation, and he just let me walk away.

"Why don't you head back to your room at the hotel and rest? Our flight leaves pretty early in the morning, and you look exhausted," my father tells me softly.

"It's still early. I don't want to leave you alone."

Ben had shown up right before we went to dinner to whisk Brooke away for some alone time before they had to say good-bye. He seemed really excited when I told him my father and I were going out to dinner on the other side of the island away from the hotel and would be gone for a few hours. I'm sure it's because their alone time would be spent in the hotel room I shared with Brooke, and I tried not to be jealous each time he gave me a wink and asked me just how long I planned on being away from my room.

At least he wasn't looking at me with pity, with my puffy, red-rimmed eyes from crying and my hair in a messy bun on top of my head because I didn't give a shit about how I looked. Although, that almost made me even sadder. If he wasn't looking at me with sympathy and understanding, that means Declan never said anything to him about me. That means Declan didn't even care about me getting off the ship and walking away. He let me go and he just went about his business as if nothing ever happened. As if he hadn't stood in that wheelhouse and told me I made him want to change all his plans.

Fuck!

I can feel the sting of tears welling up in my eyes and I know I need to get out of here before I become a sobbing mess in the middle of the restaurant.

"Mackenzie, I'll be fine," my father says, setting his napkin on the table and waving for our waitress to bring the check. "I'm just going to walk along the beach around here for a while and enjoy the rest of this beautiful weather before we head back home. Go. Get back to the hotel and relax. I'll be fine."

With an apology and a kiss on his cheek, I move quickly through the tables of the small seafood restaurant and rush outside to get a taxi to take me back to the hotel.

I was too distracted and lost in my own thoughts to notice the twinkle in my father's eye when I made my escape, or how the excited look on his face matched that of Ben's before he disappeared with Brooke earlier, and how he wouldn't stop asking when I was going back to the hotel.

I should have noticed. I should have been paying attention.

⚓

WHEN I LET myself into mine and Brooke's hotel room, I poke my head around the door slowly, happy to find it empty and not filled with the sounds of Brooke and Ben saying their goodbye's. I don't bother turning on any lights as I move into the room and let the door close behind me with a quiet *click*. I left the double balcony doors wide open before we left for dinner and the setting sun during my taxi ride back was replaced with a full moon sitting high in the sky above the water, shining through the doors and giving me enough light to see by as I make my way over to the balcony.

Stepping outside onto the ledge ten stories up from the ground, I rest my hands on the railing, take a deep breath of the salty ocean air, and let the tears fall that I'd been holding back since I left the restaurant. My head drops between my shoulders and I let myself cry one last time, getting it all out of my system before I leave here tomorrow and have to find a way to be strong and try to forget.

"Mackenzie."

A strangled cry flies out of me as I whip my head up and whirl around when I hear my name whispered softly from behind me. I don't know why I'm surprised. I could smell his soap and a soft hint of that cologne he wears as soon as I walked into the room, but I thought it was just my imagination playing tricks on me and torturing me with the memory of him. It's what made me break down into tears as soon as I got out on the balcony. The same tears that are still making tracks down my cheeks as I see him standing right in front of me in the doorway leading out onto this balcony. I swipe them away angrily, hating that he's in my room right now, seeing me so pathetic and weak, crying over him when he doesn't deserve my tears.

"Mackenzie," he whispers, saying my name again.

I ignore the flutters in my stomach that just the sound of his voice produces. I ignore the way my heart beats faster by having him so close to me I can reach out and touch him. And I ignore the way he's looking at me with a mixture of apprehension and nerves and sorrow.

His eyes are bloodshot and tired-looking, and his usually clean-shaven face is covered with dark stubble, which makes him look better than ever. I hate that I want to slide my hands down the side of his face and feel the rough scratch of his facial hair against my palms. I hate that I want to run my fingers under his tired eyes and ask him what's wrong. I hate that I can't stop myself from caring.

"Wh-what the hell are you doing here? How...how did you get in my room?" I ask angrily, crossing my arms in front of me and hating the way my voice sounds scratchy and hesitant instead of strong and pissed off.

He steps out onto the balcony with me and I drop my arms to my sides, my back smacking into the railing behind me. I'm cursing myself for coming out here and for him being in my space and not giving me anywhere to go to escape him.

"I got here right after you and your dad left for dinner. I know the owner of the hotel and he gave me a key to your room," Declan tells me quietly.

My eyes narrow when he runs one hand nervously through his hair, and I see the ends that are now sticking up all over the place are still slightly damp.

"Did you seriously take a shower in my room?" I ask angrily.

He shrugs, sliding his hands into the front pockets of his jeans before smiling at me with those fucking dimples in his cheeks.

"I kind of had a rough couple of days. I ran off the ship earlier without thinking. Ben brought me a change of clothes, and I knew you'd be gone for a while," he explains.

So that explains all the questions from Ben about how long I'd be gone from the room tonight. And my father must have been in on it as well since he was in such a hurry to get me to come back here by myself and leave him to his "walk" along the beach.

Fucking traitors.

"Great. Hope you enjoyed yourself. You can leave now," I tell him, pushing off the railing to walk around him.

His hands quickly come out of his pockets and he wraps them around my upper arms to stop me. I immediately shrug them off, jerking my body back and away from him. He doesn't get the hint and he doesn't get out of my way. He stalks towards me until I have no other choice but to move, walking backwards until I'm bumping into the railing again.

His hands grab onto the railing on either side of me, caging me in, and his body is so close to me I can feel the heat from it as his chest brushes against mine.

"I'm sorr—"

"You're sorry, you were wrong, and I was right?" I cut him off with a humorless laugh. "Save it. You don't owe me an apology. You don't owe me anything. It was just a fun vacation fling, remember? It's done. My vacation is over, and now we can both get back to our lives."

I watch with sick fascination as his Adam's apple bobs while he takes a nervous swallow. I hold my breath, wanting him to say the words I've been dreaming about even though I want to smack my hand across his face for how much he hurt me by letting me walk away.

"I never should have said what I did. About your life and not needing to work. I never should have let you go. You have no idea how awful I feel now that..."

He trails off and it suddenly hits me. Why he's here and why he felt the need to come and find me and apologize. He *knows*. I can't even bring myself to be happy that he admitted he never should have let me go. He's only sorry and he only wants me now because now he knows we're more alike than he ever thought.

"Oh, my God. You son of a bitch," I whisper, my eyes filling with tears as I stare up at him, cursing myself for thinking for even one second that he changed his mind without knowing all of the details of my life. That he realized he made a mistake before he knew just how shitty my life really is.

I shove my hands against his chest, but he doesn't move. I do it again, smacking them as hard as I can against him, wanting to get away from him before I make an even bigger fool of myself.

"Get away from me!" I sob, pushing and shoving

the solid brick wall in front of me that is Declan, who refuses to budge.

His hands remain locked tightly around the railing on either side of me and he doesn't say a word as I smack my hands against his chest, letting all the anger and frustration and pain come screaming out of me.

"So, you heard the news. You found out my life isn't as picture perfect as you made it out to be in your head and suddenly decided I was worth the trouble? You suddenly realized now that I'm not a spoiled, rich princess you could have me? FUCK YOU!" I shout, the tears falling harder and faster down my face.

Declan quickly lets go of the railing and grabs my wrists, holding them between us and stopping me from continuing to beat the hell out of him with my hands and my words when he finally speaks.

"No! That's not it at all," he argues, holding my wrists tighter and pulling me against him with a rough yank. "Yes, I saw the news this morning, but that's not why I'm here. That's not what made me try and drink myself to death ever since I let you walk away from me, and that's not what made me hate myself and replay all of the things I should have said to you every second of the last forty-eight hours!"

I close my eyes tightly, not wanting to look at him, not wanting to let myself feel anything for him. I try to pull my hands out of his grip, wanting to cover my ears so I don't have to hear the raw pain and misery in his voice when he speaks, but he won't let me go.

"I knew I was going to come and find you and beg you to forgive me as soon as I woke up this morning," he continues, moving closer, pressing my hands against his chest and holding them there.

I feel the rapid beat of his heart under my palms and I try to pull them away, but he still won't let me.

"I knew you weren't a rich, spoiled princess the first time you opened your mouth. I knew you were worth it the first time I touched you. I made a mistake, and you'll never know how fucking sorry I am I let you walk away from me," he says, his voice cracking with emotion.

I can't help it, I let my eyes slowly open and I look up at him, my heart shattering when I see the pain on his face as looks down at me, his eyes pleading with me to understand.

"I let your fucking bitch of a stepmother fill my head with shit that ate away at my insecurities and made me second-guess everything I felt for you. You were *always* worth it, Mackenzie, but she made me think *I* wasn't worthy of *you*," he tells me softly, taking a deep breath. "It didn't matter if you were the richest woman in the world or didn't have a penny to your name. All I could think about was what kind of life I could give you. You're smart, beautiful, and the most amazing woman I've ever met. You deserve *everything*, and all I can give you is a life never staying in one place, on a boat in the middle of the ocean. It scared the hell out of me that it wouldn't be enough for you. That *I* wouldn't be enough for you."

I knew something must have happened to make him go so quickly from wanting me to change his plans to not wanting me at all, but I never imagined it had anything to do with Allyson. I should have known, and it makes me hate her even more than I already do that she managed to fuck up my life in more ways than one.

"All you had to do was ask. That's all I wanted. I just wanted you to ask," I sob, my tears falling faster and harder. "I would have told you that you were worth more than anything I had waiting for me back home. I would have told you that nothing would have made me happier than spending my life never staying in one place, on a boat in the middle of the ocean with you."

He groans, dropping his head until his forehead is pressed against mine.

"Stay with me," he whispers. "Don't go. I love you, Mackenzie. I can't be on that boat without you. I can't walk around that ship without seeing you everywhere I go, without needing you there with me. I love the way you make me laugh, I love the way you make me want more out of my life. I love the way you make me happy for the first fucking time in my life. I love the way you make me feel like I could make *you* happy. I love that you make me feel like I'm enough for you, even though I know I'm not. I love everything I already know about you and everything I can't wait to learn about you. I love the way you say my name and the way you look at me, and how no matter what I do, I can't get you off my mind. I love that you've thrown me off course and that I never want to get back on track. I love you. Stay with me."

It's everything I wanted from him. It's all the words I wanted him to say, if only he'd said them before he let me walk away.

"I don't trust you, Declan. I don't trust the words you're saying no matter how much I want to. I needed them two days ago, not now, not after you know what's going on with my father and think you can make everything better by telling me what I want to hear."

He lets go of my hands and presses his palms to either side of my face, tilting my head up so I have no other choice but to look into his eyes.

"You can ask Ben. You can ask Zoe and Marcel. They were there when I told them I'd fucked up before I read the article. They were ready to kick my ass if I didn't get off that boat and come find you. Yes, I felt like the biggest asshole in the world when I found out everything you'd been dealing with and keeping to yourself, but it's not why I'm here. I know I can't make everything better. I know I can't fix everything, but I want to try. Please, stay with me," he pleads.

I shake my head in his hands and he leans down, kissing the tears off my cheeks.

"I love you. Stay with me," he whispers.

The broken pieces of my heart start slowly putting themselves back together every time he says the words I needed from him.

"Stay with me."

It stops mattering why he's here or what made him get off that ship and come find me. I can hear it in his voice, and I can see it on his face that he means every word he says.

"Stay with me."

He continues to kiss away the tears that continue to fall and I clutch the material of his t-shirt in my fists where my hands are still pressed against his chest, the steady beat of his heart still thumping under them.

I'm weak and I'm pathetic, and suddenly, I don't care. I don't care about anything but the man standing in front of me, pouring his heart out to me. I don't care that I've only known him for two weeks and in that span of time, he's broken my heart more times than I can count. All I care about is the fact that he can put it back together.

"Stay with me," he whispers one last time, pulling his lips away from my cheek to look down at me.

"How can I be sure that's what you want? How can you be sure that's what *you* want? You have a future and plans and I'm just going to mess all of that up," I tell him softly, flatting my palms against him as he leans into me, his body pressing against mine from hip to chest.

"I already told you. You make me want to change all

of my plans. You make me want the storm throwing me off course. As long as you stay with me."

He dips his head and presses his mouth to mine, holding his lips there and whispering against them one last time.

"I need you to stay with me."

I slide my hands up his chest and wrap my arms around his shoulders, locking them together behind his neck and pushing myself up on my toes.

"Prove it."

CHAPTER 27

Declan

AFTER I TOOK a shower in Mackenzie's bathroom, I had plenty of time to sit in a chair in a dark corner of the hotel room and think about everything I needed to say to her.

All the words I wanted to say fled from my mind as soon as I heard her walk in and watched her walk right by me without even noticing I was there.

All of the words I carefully thought out and planned disappeared and I couldn't do anything but say her name when the sight of her crying on the balcony almost killed me.

I hated myself for being the one to make her cry. I hated my insecurities and my weakness and for allowing someone to let me push her away and hurt her like this. I forgot everything I wanted to say, and all I could do was beg her to stay, over and over. All I could do was touch her and hold her and refuse to let her go and tell her I love her, hoping it would be enough.

As soon as she wrapped her arms around me, pushed her body up on her toes so we were closer to eye-level and told me to prove it, I forgot everything but how happy she makes me and how I never want to let her out of my sight for the rest of my life.

I crush my lips to hers, wrapping my arms tighter around her and lifting her body up against mine. Our mouths open at the same time and I groan into her when I feel the first slide of her tongue against mine. Turning her away from the railing of the balcony, I swirl my tongue deeper into her mouth, pouring everything I have into this kiss as I walk us a few steps until I'm pushing her up against the wall next to the open balcony doors.

My hands are everywhere all at once, needing to touch every inch of her and prove to myself that this isn't a dream. That she's really here, in my arms, letting me love her and letting me prove to her that I meant every word I said.

"I love you. Stay with me," I whisper again, kissing my way down the side of her neck as my hands move up and under the edge of her shirt, sliding against the soft, smooth skin of her sides.

My teeth gently nip at the skin where her neck meets her shoulder, and I hear her head thump back against the wall as I run my tongue over that spot. My hands quickly move up under her shirt until I'm pushing her bra up and out of the way and finally have her breasts in my hands.

She moans my name when I knead them in my palms and rub my thumbs over her hardened nipples, the sound of my name on her lips making my dick swell and thicken in my pants. I bend my knees and then push up between her legs, lifting her off the ground as she wraps her legs around my waist. I push myself against her core, needing her to feel how much I want her.

How much I need her, and how much I love what she does to me.

With her legs wrapped tightly around me, I thrust my hips between her thighs, pushing her higher up the wall and rubbing my cock against her, aching for her and needing her so much I can't think straight.

She removes her arms from around my shoulders long enough to help me yank her shirt up and over her head, tossing it to the side before wrapping my hands around her breasts again, pushing them up as I dip my head and circle my tongue around one nipple.

"Stay with me," I whisper against her, before wrapping my lips around her nipple and sucking it hard, into my mouth.

Her fingers slide through my hair, clutching the short strands into her fists and holding me in place as I suck and lick and torture her with my tongue. Her hips start moving as she moans in pleasure, sliding herself over my cock that is so fucking hard I feel like I'm going to lose my mind if I don't get inside of her soon.

I need her. I want her. I love her, but I won't take what I want until she gives me the words.

"Stay with me," I demand softly, pulling my mouth away from her breast and standing up straighter so I can see her face as I slide my hands up her bare thighs.

Her hips are still moving, rubbing against my cock, and I grab her hip in one hand to hold it still, and pull myself back just enough to slip my other hand between her thighs.

I stare into her eyes as I tug aside the cotton material of her shorts and the tips of my fingers come in contact with her hot, wet skin.

"Stay with me," I beg, watching her lips part with a gasp and her eyes glaze over with lust when I plunge two fingers inside of her tight heat, hard and fast.

I slide my hand off her hip and move it around to her lower back, wrapping my arm around her and pulling her closer as I fuck my fingers into her, bringing my thumb up to gently circle around her swollen clit.

She rocks her hips against my hand, pulling my fingers in deeper, forcing my thumb to brush against her clit harder until she's whimpering my name with every breath she takes.

One of her arms flies down from around my shoulder and she wedges it between us, bending her knees and spreading her legs wider to make room for both of our hands as I continue pumping my fingers in and out of her and she quickly undoes my jeans.

It's my turn to moan her name loudly when I feel her hand wrap around my cock, pulling it out of my pants and squeezing it as she runs her palm up and down the length.

When her thumb rubs over the head of my cock, spreading pre-come all around the tip, I jerk my fingers out of her and shove her hand away, replacing it with my own as I hold myself in my fist and slide my cock through her wetness.

She moves her fingers between her legs, spreading her shorts open wider for me, tightening her thighs around my waist and bringing me closer until my cock is pressed right up against her opening.

Her arm bands tighter around my shoulder until her breasts are pressed flat against my chest and I can feel her nipples through my shirt. She rocks her hips again and the head of my cock inches inside her. I squeeze my hand tighter around the base and refuse to push myself inside her until I hear the words.

"Stay. With. Me," I tell her, each word punctuated with a swipe of the head of my cock over her clit.

"Fuck me, Declan," she moans, her legs practically cutting off my circulation with how tightly she's clenching her thighs around me, trying to pull me inside of her.

My cock jumps in my hand, and I know I'm going to come all over her pussy in about two seconds instead of doing it buried deep inside of her, where I want to be. Where I *need* to be.

"Just say the words, and I will, baby," I reassure her, counting to ten in my head as I continue pushing and sliding my cock through her wetness. "Stay with me."

I watch her eyes fill with tears as she looks at me. I watch one of them escape and fall down her cheek. I let go of my cock, pushing my hips forward and holding myself against her to bring my hand up to her face and cup it in my hand, swiping the tear away with my thumb.

"Mackenzie, please. Stay with me."

She brings her hand up from between us and presses it on top of mine against her cheek, looking into my eyes, searching between them until she finally sees the truth I needed her to.

"Yes," she finally whispers back.

With a groan of relief, I pull my hips back and then push myself inside of her, slowly, until my cock is so deep I don't know where I end and she begins. It's cliché as fuck and I don't care. I want her to be my beginning and I want her to be my end.

"I love you," I mutter against her mouth before pressing my lips to hers and sliding my tongue inside.

Both of her arms come back around my shoulders and both of mine wrap tightly around her body as I thrust my cock in and out of her in a gentle rhythm. She gives me her body against the wall of the balcony, and I take everything she has, knowing I'll do whatever it takes for the rest of my life to show her she isn't making a mistake.

Each time I pull my cock out of her and slowly ease back inside her body, I hold myself deep and grind myself against her, rubbing her clit with my groin until she's digging her nails into my back and the heels of her bare feet into my ass.

I pick up my pace, fucking her harder, slamming into her rougher, unable to stop my release from tightening my balls with how good she feels wrapped around me.

She chants my name as I drive into her, telling me she's coming, and I feel her pussy tighten and clench, squeezing my cock as a rush of wetness from her release stimulates my own and throws me over the edge. I thrust into her one last time and hold myself deep, coming inside the woman who, in just a few weeks' time became my entire world, as I shout her name, not giving a shit that we're outside on a balcony and anyone can hear me.

My body slumps against hers and I continue holding her up against the wall, our foreheads pressed together as we both pant and try to catch our breaths. I refuse to pull myself out of her body.

"I'll stay," Mackenzie whispers, the sound of those

words making my dick jump while it's still buried inside of her.

I pull my head away from hers and remove one of my arms from around her waist to brush a strand of hair out of her eyes as I stare down at her and smile.

"But not until you say what I need to hear," she adds, her eyes sparkling and her mouth tipping up into a mischievous grin.

I laugh softly as she raises one eyebrow and waits for me to say the words she needs.

"You're right. I was wrong. And I'm sorry," I tell her with a complete look of seriousness on my face.

I knew the moment Mackenzie Armstrong walked onto the ship that my life would change forever, but I had no idea just how much I would enjoy every minute of it and not care one bit about having to change my course.

"You're forgiven," Mackenzie whispers with a smile, sliding her hands to the back of my head and pulling my mouth to hers.

EPILOGUE

Two years later...

"**D**AMN, THEY MADE the front page. Very impressive. Read it to me, wife."

Brooke laughs at her husband of six months as he tosses her a copy of the *Miami Herald*, then flops down on the couch and rests his head in her lap.

Brooke never thought in a million years she'd meet a man-whore on vacation and wind up becoming his wife, but here they are, living in Florida. She relocated and got a job in his home town, and quickly realized married life is a piece of cake when you're husband leaves for seventeen weeks at a time to work on a yacht and you aren't constantly at each other's throats.

"Ben, don't make me punch you," she threatens, unfolding the paper above his head and smiling at the article that takes up the entire front page. "You only have about an hour before you need to get down on the docks and get to work on the new boat. I'd much rather spend it naked than beating the shit out of you."

Ben laughs, making himself more comfortable by kicking his feet up on the arm of the couch as she starts to read the interview about their friends, and the new boat Ben is leaving to work on later today.

> Miami locals came out in droves today to see the inaugural christening of the newly refurbished, 150-foot luxury yacht, named Vacation Fling, anxiously wait for it to lift anchor later today, and set out on its first charter towards the US Virgin Islands. Miami has been glued to the docks for the last few months, watching the ship get a face-lift, proud to see one of their own, Captain Declan McGillis, behind the wheel.
>
> Captain McGillis, who has been in charge of running charters on luxury yachts ever since he obtained his captain's license almost two years ago, sat down with us before he and his crew set sail to answer some of our questions.
>
> Vacation Fling is unlike any other luxury yacht, in that the crew quarters down below offer the same beautiful opulence as the guest quarters up top.
>
> "I want my crew to know they're just as important. I want them to be comfortable and not feel like they're any less deserving of the things offered to the guests. I want them to love their jobs, and I want them to keep coming back every charter season," Captain McGillis told us.
>
> Also unlike any other luxury yacht, Captain McGillis was given cart blanche on all the changes made to the refurbished ship before its first charter, and he doesn't shy away from shooting down the naysayers who think he was only hired as the captain because of who the owner of the

yacht is.

"I know people think I had it made considering my father-in-law owns the ship,
but Mark Armstrong doesn't let anyone walk
all over him. He's been through a lot, and
he's one of the strongest men I know. He
didn't hand me this job just because I'm
married to his daughter. I had to work my
ass off and prove myself, just like any other captain, and I wouldn't have it any other
way."

Mark Armstrong, making national news
two years ago for filing bankruptcy after
his wife of one year was found to have stolen the majority of the fortune he'd made in
the software application industry, paid a
hefty price for his error in judgment, by
not only losing all of the money he'd made
developing one of the world's most popular
dating apps, but by also losing the company
he built from the ground up.

Luckily, Mr. Armstrong's talents with
computer programming weren't stolen from
him as well, and he made double the amount
he did selling his first app, when he sold
the rights a year ago for a new app, Digging
for Gold. This dating app is unlike any
other on the market, in that it's geared
specifically to individuals in a certain
tax bracket, who are looking for a love
that will not bleed them dry and make them
fall victim to financial ruin, like Mr.
Armstrong.

When asked why the ship was named Vacation Fling, Captain McGillis shared a
smile with his wife, Mackenzie McGillis,
and told us it was an inside joke. It's hard
not to feel like a third wheel watching the

two of them sit side-by-side at the formal dining table on Vacation Fling, constantly smiling at each other, reaching for the others hand or seeing them whisper in each other's ear and laugh together. Love is in the ocean air on Vacation Fling, and the stress of starting a new charter season doesn't seem to be affecting either of them.

Mr. and Mrs. McGillis have worked side-by-side on luxury yachts ever since they met two years ago when Mackenzie's father chartered the boat Captain McGillis worked on. As a ship photographer, capturing all of the guest's moments on board, and as well as the activity planner making sure the guests enjoy every moment during their charter and ensuring the excursions they take off the ship run smoothly, Mackenzie McGillis says there's nothing else she'd rather do than spend her time on a boat, traveling the world with her husband.

"I was a little lost and unsure of my future when I got on board my first yacht two years ago. And then I met Declan and everything changed. I fell in love and I found what made me happy. Watching his dreams come true, being a part of it and being there every step of the way...I've never been more proud of him than I am right now. I've never been happier that he asked me to stay, and I did."

The couple married exactly one year ago today, on another luxury yacht called the Helios, the same ship where they met, fell in love, and proceeded to work together.

"It just seemed right that we get married out in the middle of the ocean where we first met. Mackenzie once told me she wasn't looking for a white picket fence or for me to throw away all my hopes and dreams. So, I gave her a white deck railing and I made her part of my hopes and dreams. And now we get to spend our first anniversary doing what we love, on a ship we poured our heart and soul into making perfect for everyone who gets on board."

We asked Mackenzie if she had any contact with the women who left her father's life in ruins and she shook her head and shrugged.

"Last I heard, Allyson did her time in jail, and now she's working a crappy job that makes her miserable just to pay the bills. Her daughter was cleared of all charges back then, and rumor has it she tried to follow in her mother's footsteps and land herself her own wealthy man, but her reputation was ruined by that point, and no one wanted anything to do with her. Other than that, I don't really care what they're doing or where they are. My father has moved on, he's rebuilt his life and now he's dating a wonderful woman, the same age as him, who has her own money and spoils him rotten. As long as he's happy, I'm happy."

When asked about the struggles of being married and working together, the couple laughed, and Captain McGillis pointed to the t-shirt he wore.

"We have our moments, just like any couple. But my wife had this shirt made for me before we got back on board the Helios two years ago and I convinced my captain at the time to let her stay and work. This shirt is all the reminder I need to never take anything for granted and to appreciate how lucky I am that Mackenzie decided to stay."

The white t-shirt Captain McGillis wears, has the words "You're right. I was wrong. I'm sorry." printed across the chest in dark blue ink, and we can only assume it's another inside joke the happy couple shares as we watch them wrap their arms around each other and share a kiss, and we bid them good luck on their maiden voyage on the Vacation Fling.

The End

If you'd like to read more of Tara's books, check out her website:

tarasivec.com

ACKNOWLEDGEMENTS

I have some pretty kick ass beta readers, and without them, I would have lost my mind completely while plotting and writing this book. Thank you to C.C. Wood, Michelle Kannan and Jessica Prince. I'm #sorrynotsorry if I made you insane while writing this thing.

Thank you to Joanne Christenson for suggesting the name Declan. Obviously it's perfect. Below Steven never would have worked.

Thank you to the best agent in all the land, Kimberly Brower. If you hadn't suggested I could swap this book idea for a different one I was supposed to write, I'd probably be dead right now. Or still in the corner, rocking back and forth in the fetal position.

Thank you to Christina Nicole and your awesome cousin Sandrine, for the French translations help. Without the two of you, "I want you so much" might have said "The purple goat eats dick cheese on the trumpet."

Thank you to all the members of Tara's Tramps for always being amazing, supportive and bat shit crazy, just like me.

Thank you to the crew of the reality TV show, Below Deck. Without my obsession with your show, this book would have never come to be. And Kelley Johnson, if you're reading this, you're like, really pretty. And you were my muse for Declan, so thank you for the eye candy.

Last, but not least, thank you to my husband and kids for letting me completely ignore you for a few weeks, and not get too mad when I don't hear a word you say, make you repeat things 800 times, and sometimes forget who you are and why you're living in my house. I love you the best.

CPSIA information can be obtained
at www.ICGtesting.com
Printed in the USA
FFOW03n1609100517
35366FF